Guardian of the Heart

a Night Stalkers CSAR romance novella
by
M. L. Buchman

Cover images:
Lighthouse Sunset © pieterpater
U.S. Army UH-60 Black Hawk helicopter ©
Michael Kaplan

Buchman Bookworks

Other works by M.L. Buchman

MAIN FLIGHT

The Night Is Mine
I Own the Dawn
Wait Until Dark
Take Over at Midnight
Light Up the Night
Bring On the Dusk
By Break of Day

WHITE HOUSE HOLIDAY

Daniel's Christmas
Frank's Independence Day
Peter's Christmas
Zachary's Christmas
Roy's Independence Day
Damien's Christmas

AND THE NAVY

Christmas at Steel Beach
Christmas at Peleliu Cove

5E

Target of the Heart
Target Lock on Love
Target of Mine

Target Engaged
Heart Strike

<u>Firehawks</u>

MAIN FLIGHT
Pure Heat
Full Blaze
Hot Point
Flash of Fire
Wild Fire

SMOKEJUMPERS
Wildfire at Dawn
Wildfire at Larch Creek
Wildfire on the Skagit

<u>Angelo's Hearth</u>
Where Dreams are Born
Where Dreams Reside
Maria's Christmas Table
Where Dreams Unfold
Where Dreams Are Written

<u>Eagle Cove</u>
Return to Eagle Cove
Recipe for Eagle Cove
Longing for Eagle Cove
Keepsake for Eagle Cove

<u>Henderson's Ranch</u>
Nathan's Big Sky

<u>Deities Anonymous</u>
Cookbook from Hell: Reheated
Saviors 101

Don't Miss a Thing!

Sign up for M. L. Buchman's newsletter
today
and receive:
Release News
Free Short Stories
a Free Starter Library

Do it today. Do it now.

http://www.mlbuchman.com/newsletter/

Chapter 1

"*Don't be looking at* her, Jones! Are you crazy, man?"

Master Sergeant Mason "The Jar" Buckley (he was kind of short and barrel-chested) yanked hard enough on Xavier's safety harness to almost knock him down on the hangar's floor. They were buddy-checking their gear before saddling up onto a Black Hawk helicopter headed way out into hell-and-gone ISIS country. Even though the overheads weren't very bright, the darkness of Iraq's Balad Air Base was like a black door across the hangar's maw.

The Jar yanked Xavier's harness the other way. Maybe Mason didn't like his sucky nickname (Xavier had one he hated with a passion and could only hope he'd finally left Stateside). Maybe Mason had it in for new guys to the unit; perhaps he was just trying to make his point.

Another possibility: maybe The Jar was an asshole.

"Why? She yours? Can't hurt a guy to look," Xavier didn't appreciate the manhandling. There was no need to bust his ass *before* he went aloft. Besides, the medic on the other side of the brightly lit hangar—shouldering a pack clearly labeled "Medical"—was well worth a second look, and a third. She was lightly built, but pulled on forty pounds of gear like it weighed nothing more than feather pillows. She wasn't model material, more the hottest-girl-in-school type—the one so hot that no one ever stood a chance. Thick black hair that fell straight to her shoulders, coffee-and-cream skin, and an attitude like kick-ass sunshine after a long winter.

"Hell no!" Masson looked aghast. "She's not mine. She's not anybody's. That's the Guardian of the Night—the goddamn Angel of Death. You don't want her evil eye on you. Bad luck, brother. Seriously bad luck." Mason picked up the FN-SCAR combat rifle from the table and slammed it against Xavier's chest.

Xavier slipped the strap around his neck and made sure it hung out of the way across his chest.

"Dude's right, you know," one of the pilots, also donning his kit, leaned over. "Something about her is way different." Then he and his copilot jogged toward the darkness.

"You're still lookin."

"Didn't know they built women like her." Where Xavier came from the women were either jovial mamas with the best kinda curves on the planet (even when they got all out of control they were still mighty good) or they were lean (like anorexic crackhead lean) and mean (big on the mean). This one stood five-eight on a tall day, athlete's curves rather than a plus-size model's, and was joking with another medic as they moved off toward the waiting helo, disappearing into the darkness.

"They don't build women like her anywhere," Mason continued but still wasn't looking where she'd gone. "Nobody's that scary."

"What? The evil eye, Angel of Death crap?" When Xavier was done with crosschecking Mason, he slammed Mason's rifle into his chest just as hard as Mason had into him.

Mason only nodded fiercely. Man looked spooked, which didn't seem right on a master sergeant of the Night Stalkers.

Xavier tapped at each of the pouches on his own vest to make sure nothing was missing: magazines for his sidearm, mags for his rifle, small med kit of his own, spare batteries for his night-vision goggles and radio, the NVGs and radio themselves. He counted items but came up one short.

He did it again, then figured out what he was missing when he slapped his own head. Helmet.

Sitting right there on the table. Damn! First day on the job, he seriously wanted to perform, not be some fresh-meat laughing stock. He'd had enough of that six years earlier on his first tour, enough to last a lifetime. However, after three full tours, he was the newest recruit again.

Transitioning from a seasoned regular Army grunt to a fresh-out-of-training Special Operations Forces Army grunt had probably reset a whole block of his don't-mess-with-me privileges. Now, after the toughest application process outside of Delta Force and two more years of training, he was finally FMQ—fully mission qualified—for the Night Stalkers of the 160th SOAR.

Maybe Mason had a point on at least one count: the woman had distracted him. In a full vest, flightsuit, and Army boots, she still looked amazing. Just the way she walked: happy to be here, belonging-where-she-was, whole spring-in-her-step kind of thing. He guessed that alone set her outside the norm for central Iraq.

He grabbed his helmet and set off at a jog beside Mason, out of the brightly lit hangar and onto the night-shrouded tarmac toward the rescue bird.

Elsewhere across the field, other helos were roaring to life. Four Black Hawks, a massive Chinook, and a couple Little Birds. The Night Stalkers were going out in force tonight, which was so sweet for a first mission. And if everything went right, he'd be bored out of his gourd— because that's what every CSAR flight wanted to be.

Combat Search and Rescue was about going into the guts of the fight and hauling out whoever had caught the worst of it. A CSAR's ideal mission was when they circled for hours out past the five-minute hold line and never got the call.

But if the hot lady and her companion had to go in, he and Mason were there to keep them safe. Xavier liked running protection detail. He didn't mind the battle when he was in it, but he preferred the far less glorious role of rescuing the wounded. He never gave it much thought, and jogging up to his bird for the first time wasn't when a dude should start thinking.

The Black Hawk waiting for them wasn't some standard Geneva Agreement-Red Cross bearing-and-no-mounted-weapons bird. It was ten tons of pitch black nasty with a pair of side-mounted M134 Miniguns that could lay down six thousand rounds of havoc per minute.

Army, Navy, Air Force's 724th Pararescue—all those guys flew air ambulances that had to be marked clearly by international treaty and were forbidden to carry any but light personal weapons for protection only. It rankled that so many of the bad guys thought the big red cross was to make their targeting easier, but the US followed the rules in this even if many of the forces it faced didn't. Of course there was no law against a pair of fully-loaded Apaches or Cobras hovering on close guard—which was standard operating practice for most teams.

Most of the Spec Ops teams depended on the 724th Pararescue to drag out the wounded. But for the Night Stalkers, they were typically so far past the enemy's (or a supposed friendly's) line that there was no way for the Air Force to get to them in time. So, of all the spec ops outfits, only the 160th SOAR lofted their own CSAR med teams.

As the helicopter transport team for Delta Force, SEAL Team 6, and the 75th Rangers—the Night Stalkers flew under different rules by definition. They always flew into the heart of the battle, well past the lines where anyone would pay attention to whether or not it was a medical flight.

Glory hounds never made it to the Night Stalkers and Xavier was good with that. Too many from the old neighborhood cared more about their "reps" than their lives. Doofuses.

So, instead of air ambulances ready to launch at a moment's notice, SOAR sent their own well-armed warbirds—ones that just happened to carry medics. The medheads were soldiers first and wore no Red Cross armbands of supposed "protection." But they had the training and carried enough gear that they could do almost anything, including open heart surgery if necessary. The Black Hawks went in armed just to make sure they stayed safe.

"What's our op tempo?" he asked Mason as they secured their gear inside their bird.

"You like the ground?"

Xavier shrugged, not knowing what he was after.

"Better kiss it goodbye. Won't be seeing it much until you rotate back stateside."

"I don't mean the regiment. I mean us, CSAR."

For a guy who talked so much, Mason's sudden silence was eloquent.

Shit!

* * *

Noreen Wallace watched the new guy. Hard to miss. He stood half a head taller than The Jar and a shoulder wider—he was as big as her older brother, maybe even bigger. Her brother wore his curly hair short, despite her teasing him to cut it off so that he'd look like Luther in the *Mission Impossible* movies—Ving Rhames might be old, but he was still a total stud.

This guy's head was smooth-shaved like Ving's. But trotting along in full combat gear made him look way more powerful than any mere movie star ever could.

He moved at a brisk pace and made it look easy. You didn't make it into Spec Ops without a lot of running, but he *looked* like a runner: smooth and fast despite his heavy load.

Barry started calling out the list and she turned to check the gear hanging on every inside surface of the Black Hawk's cargo bay: blood supply in the cooler, saline and antibiotics fully restocked, bandages okay in seven different sizes from cut to catastrophic. Barry read over a hundred items off the checklist and she verified every one—didn't even have to search to find them, their position was long since hardwired into her nervous system.

The Jar and the new guy were preflighting the helo. Both moved with the smooth efficiency of long practice.

He kept an eye on her, but kept his words to himself as he worked.

Within three minutes, the crew chiefs were aboard and checking their guns while the pilot and copilot started up the engines. As soon as they fed her power, she and Barry checked the heart monitors, defib, and IV infusion pumps.

New Guy finished his preparations just as she finished item #103: water bottle to stay hydrated in the parching desert that had once been northern Iraq but now was simply a disaster.

They turned toward each other at the same moment. He didn't balk or act awkwardly. Instead he held out a hand that completely enveloped hers when they shook.

"Guardian of the Night, huh? Or do you prefer Angel of Death?"

So, The Jar had already been telling him stories and he hadn't shied off. Good sign there. Though if she could think of a worse name to stick The Jar with, she'd do it. "Jar Jar Binks" maybe? Tempting, but that would be downright nasty. Not her style. She had fun teasing the Master Sergeant, but didn't want to hurt him.

"Stick with Guardian and we'll get on fine. Though you missed 'The Bitch of Black Death' and—" She shrugged. A long litany of nicknames had marked her past, like mile markers on the highway; this was only the latest.

He smiled rather than backing away. "Guessin' you kinda forced 'Guardian of the Night' down their throats."

"Got it in one."

His smile was a dazzler, and there was no doubt that he knew it. This was *not* her brother John. John was the big-hearted storyteller of any crowd with an eager laugh and a soft manner—behind which hid the Number Two mechanic in the Night Stalkers. He was the first to acknowledge that his wife, Connie, ranked Number One—whose shy smiles were so rare that Noreen sometimes teased her fair-skinned sister-in-law that it was time to start cataloging them.

"You got a name or do I just call you Guardian?"

"Lieutenant Noreen Wallace. You?"

"Staff Sergeant Xavier Jones."

She could see him wince ever so slightly, as if his name hurt him.

No, it would be the obvious nickname: The X-Man. Or Mister Egghead. Both were bad and inevitable—and way too obvious. Professor X, Charles Xavier, the bald leader of the comic book X-Men. Xavier looked the role: massive and imposing in a way that a little white guy like Patrick Stewart only pulled off in the movies by being so smart. Sergeant Jones's power was out there for all to see.

"Nice to meet you, 'Captain Luc.'" She waited while he blinked once, twice, then tugged down on his Kevlar vest the same way Patrick Stewart always had tugged his uniform as Captain Jean-Luc Picard of Star Trek's *Enterprise.*

"Pleased to meet you, Miss Guardian," he said in his big deep voice, with all of the formality a starship captain would have used.

She laughed and he grinned back at her. You had to be more than just sharp to make it into the Night Stalkers. You had to be smart as hell. And to get a pass from her, a background in comics and science fiction was essential.

The helo lifted, and she and Barry slid the side doors of the Black Hawk's cargo bay closed.

Xavier swung into his seat, snapped his vest to the safety harness, and yanked his helmet's visor down. Even behind all that gear, he still stood out for his sheer size. It was a wonder he could cram into the tight gunner's seat at all.

As with every flight, she sent a prayer aloft to whoever was listening that she'd have no work tonight. A prayer that was answered far too rarely.

* * *

Xavier sat facing sideways behind the pilot seat, his Minigun on an armature that reached out through the hull and offered a wide range of fire in defense of the bird.

He watched the tactical display running across the inside of his visor. The main flight was in the lead by twenty kilometers and five minutes. They were down at NOE. Nap-of-Earth flight was better than the best roller coaster at the county fair, and nobody flew the track like a Night Stalker pilot. Ten tons of helo zipped along less than fifty feet above the ground: hugging hills, slicing past trees, dodging houses.

He kept his hands firmly on his Minigun's handles, using it and his harness for bracing. The mission briefing had said they were flying through the Zagros Mountains where they'd gotten word of a large terrorist team on the move. He'd done six half-year deployments during his previous three tours and knew this part of Northeastern Iraq too well. It was like coming home—to a nightmare, but as much of a home as he'd ever had.

"Beats the shit out of Mobile," he mumbled to himself, then heard it in the headphones built into his helmet. Open intercom.

" 'Bama boy?" the male medic asked.

"Army boy," was all Xavier was now.

"Name is Barry, if anyone cares."

"Sorry, Barry. My bad. Noreen's such a damn dazzler. Don't know how you can form a coherent sentence working alongside someone like that."

"Hey, I'm right here listening."

"Yes, ma'am." Wouldn't have been any point in teasing her if she wasn't.

"Don't I know it. I feel invisible around

her," Barry had an easy sense of humor, which Xavier liked about him. "And everybody's from somewhere."

"Not me." Xavier wasn't quite sure how to bull his way out of this one—not bullshit, but rather bull in china shop to get away from the topic. "Born in the Army."

"You got a name, or do I just call you Rookie?"

"Sorry, dude. Name is Xavier Jo—"

"Captain Luc," Noreen declared. "Cap'n for short."

"Name is Cap'n Luc," Xavier tried not to miss a beat, "nice rank bump there. And I'm from nowhere. I got beamed aboard when I hit Fort Benning for Basic Training. Rest of before that…" he shuddered. Rest of before that he did his best to never think about.

The two medics sat in jump seats at the back of the cargo bay. Funny how far away ten feet felt when his other side was rubbing against the back of the pilot's seat.

"Why Guardian of the Night?" he asked over the intercom, wondering how such a pleasant woman struck such terror into an old hand like the master sergeant.

"Angel of Death," The Jar groaned like a lost soul.

"I answer to both," Noreen happily agreed.

Xavier liked her voice, a winning combination of warmth and sass. He'd spent three months working with a British team in Baghdad during his second deployment. Cyril would have called her cheeky—it worked on her.

"Why?"

"You'll see," Mason sounded grim.

"Should have been a dwarf named Mopey for you, Mason."

The master sergeant growled, reminding Xavier exactly who outranked him here—everybody.

But Noreen's bright laugh told him it was worth the price he was bound to pay.

Chapter 2

The call came less than five minutes into the battle.

Actually, by the time the call came in, they were already on the move. Noreen had heard the feed from enough battles to know the moment one went sideways.

"Go!" was all she had to shout. Vince and Penny had flown with her long enough to stop questioning her diagnoses. They just laid down the hammer and the Black Hawk jumped as if it had been kicked like a football.

The call officially came in twenty seconds after they were on the move. Per usual, it was: dead calm, matter-of-fact, and with about a tenth of the information she needed. Air Mission Commanders didn't get flustered in the middle of battle any more than the fighters they were commanding, but they also were usually occupied with more problems than a hurt soldier when a battle took a bad turn.

"Two men down," and a set of battle coordinates.

Were they on the flat ground or cliff side? The heart of the Zagros Mountains had plenty of both. Was it a small helo down or shot-up US Rangers who'd been riding in the belly of the Chinook? Surrounded by enemies, or safely behind the main team?

Assume terrible and plan for something worse. Her sister-in-law might be a mechanic, but it didn't mean she had the rule wrong for a medic.

Noreen shrugged on her small pack—the ten-pounder of the bare essentials. Over the years, she'd been watching the Delta Force operators. When they went into a battle zone, they didn't go in like the US Rangers with loads of gear. They carried the absolute minimum, along with as much ammo as they could manage. That was a Delta Force operator's idea of traveling light— five pounds of survival gear and forty pounds of ammo.

The full med-kit weighed too much if she had to help carry or drag a soldier back to the bird—it slowed her down. Piece by precious piece she'd pared her primary field kit in half, then half again, and lived in terror of the day she'd learn a bad lesson about what she'd left behind on the helo. She always had the full kit ready and waiting just in case she changed her mind at the last second.

"One minute," Vince "Cruiser" Jawolski (who only looked a little like his hero Tom Cruise) called out. "Boulder country. Close."

Boulders meant there probably wouldn't be a way to land the helo. She'd grabbed a stretcher, but now tossed it aside.

Close meant close to enemy fire. Vince would have to drop them off, dodge away for safety, then circle back when she was ready for extraction.

"Ropes?" The new guy asked, as if she didn't know how to kick out her own Fast Rope. Nice of him to ask though. Overly macho, but nice.

Noreen leaned her head out the door to look into the night. Her night-vision goggles showed the battle zone in a hundred shades of green. Long rips of gunfire from the helicopters circling above. The occasional bold streak of a missile leaving a hot trail across her field of vision, then ending in a bright bloom of destruction when it hit an enemy position.

Ground fire pounded upward. Big, bright lines of anti-aircraft. Small, nasty slices from AK-47s and the like. No sign of RPGs. No bright flare of a fire near a downed bird.

US ground troops, clearly marked by the infrared-reflective tabs on their uniforms, were spread out across the boulder field and moving forward under heavy fire.

"Low and quiet," she called back.

Captain Luc swung his Minigun into position.

"Quiet means don't fire unless you have to," she called out.

"I know what the hell it means, sister," his snarl said that, in addition to his pretty smile, he had a mean-as-hell battle mode. "Just wanta be in position to save your fine ass if I need to."

And that actually made her laugh. She normally hated it when someone separated her from the crowd for being female, but he'd made it sound like a high compliment and that tickled her.

"Barry has a fine ass, too," she countered as she searched for the injured team.

"Was wondering when you'd notice," Barry would be searching out the other side.

"Two o'clock, a hundred yards out." The first to spot the wounded, Xavier's voice was abruptly pure business.

Noreen checked and didn't see anything. And then she realized, that was the point: she *didn't* see anything. A couple of human-sized heat signatures, but no gunfire from their position. Captain Luc had potential.

"Do it!"

* * *

Xavier had expected the pilot to fly forward. Instead, he dropped from twenty feet above the boulder field to ten. Before he could drop any farther, Noreen jumped. At five feet, Barry followed but he was already well behind her.

Noreen had landed on one boulder, but let her momentum shift and send her leaping onto the next. She hit a flat rock in a long dive, then swung her legs around like a vault over a pommel horse before moving to the next.

Even as the pilots began pulling back, Noreen reached the wounded soldiers.

"What the hell?" He'd never seen anything like it.

"Parkour," Mason told him, even though he'd been facing the other way over his own side-facing Minigun. "You know those guys who climb walls and jump from rooftop to rooftop with no special gear? She got all trained up in that."

"I've never seen anyone move so fast over a landscape."

He saw Barry finally catch up with her and they huddled down over the two men lying among the boulders.

That's when Xavier spotted enemy troops climbing a cliff wall to the south. They were trying to get into position above the med team. Not wanting to attract way too much attention to their CSAR bird by using his Minigun, he swung his FN-SCAR rifle up from his chest.

He lined up over the Minigun, checked the angle to make sure he wasn't going to shoot the spinning rotor blades of his own damned helo, and fired three-round bursts.

The first was low and right. The second took out the man to the left, the third nailed the bastard with his rifle aimed down into the battlefield below.

Xavier could see that he got off a single round, which sparked rock not two feet from Noreen's head. He didn't live long enough to shoot off a second.

Noreen didn't even bother to look up at the distraction though she must have heard it. Barry flinched badly though he was farther away. That was one cool-headed chick.

The battle line surged back and forth, helos raining down brilliant arcs of fire. At least they were brilliant in his night-vision gear—without NVGs, they would fall like invisible death upon the enemy's heads. The anti-aircraft fire made his palms itch.

He should be shooting those bastards, he had a decent angle—okay, a kinda decent angle—on them. But that would draw fire to the CSAR bird. Once they were involved in the fray, it would be much harder to break off and go for the extraction. Their best move was to stay low and quiet in the background.

The ground team had to call for an extraction at some point. Then he could lay a ring of death if necessary. He safetied and let his rifle hang once more against his chest. Then he grabbed the Minigun's handles. Next perp who messed with their med team was going to get a hundred-round burst in the face rather than just three.

"Told you," Mason spoke up over the intercom.

"Angel of Death. She's just keeping us hanging here like she was out on a Sunday stroll."

"Or until she thinks it safe to transport the guy."

"You'll see," was the sergeant's dire prediction. He obviously wasn't the cheerful sort. "We should already have them aboard and be outta here."

"You're still flying CSAR," Xavier spotted a potential threat, but so did a passing Little Bird attack helo that blew the crap out of it.

After a long silence and a short gun burst, Mason responded. "I like saving our guys. It's a good thing. But the Angel of Death—shouldn't have called her that, definitely not to her face—is some kind of extreme."

Some kind of extreme. Made Xavier wonder if that carried over into other parts of her life. He was most of the way to a pleasant fantasy when he spotted a problem.

They'd been circling a mile outside the battle zone. At the moment, he was facing out toward what should have been empty night, but it wasn't.

"Trouble at four o'clock," he called to the pilots. "Coming up the road fast."

The pilot twisted the helo's nose to face the incoming traffic, which let both him and Mason line up on them simultaneously by leaning out their windows and aiming forward.

It was a line of vehicles. Out here, it wouldn't be theirs. And they were coming up from behind the US lines. The rearmost position of the US offensive right now was defined by their medics.

"Engage or extract?" He knew what his answer would be, but it wasn't his call.

One of the pilots got on the radio with the Air Mission Commander flying somewhere high, maybe even back at base and watching through a drone.

"Engage!"

Shit! If something went wrong, the med team would be added to tonight's casualty list. Now it was his job to make sure that they weren't.

He lined up on the lead vehicle and pulled the trigger.

* * *

"Uh-oh! That's not right!" Noreen twisted to look east into the night. All of tonight's action had been to the west, except for those shooters that she could just feel Xavier was responsible for eliminating.

The hard, heavy, chainsaw *brap!* of a pair of Miniguns to the east meant they were now surrounded.

She stared down at the Ranger she'd been unable to save. Lifting him to a helicopter would have eliminated what little chance he had, but not even all the gear aboard would have saved him in time.

His buddy was alternately begging his friend to wake up and screaming at her. When he grabbed the front of her flight vest to shake her, she sighed—then leaned a calf gently against the shattered knee he was too hyped to notice. Sometimes it took a bit to burn a hole through a wall of panic.

Thankfully, it took only that little pressure to get his undivided attention. He released her and collapsed back.

She glanced again to the east and saw that their own flight out was fully engaged in the battle. Now came the thing she hated the most. She'd signed up to save lives, not take them.

Noreen slammed the injured Ranger's rifle into his hands and shouted, "Saddle up, soldier. We've got unfriendly incoming." His Ranger brain knew what to do with that.

She slapped a morphine ampule into his thigh to deaden the shattered knee. Barry had already stabilized it with a splint and bandage—nothing arterial, but he'd probably need a new joint.

Taking the dead Ranger's rifle, she knelt beside Barry with his handgun out, and the three of them peered around the shielding boulder. Back on the farm, her big brother had made sure that she was an excellent shot, even before she'd gone Army ROTC. She had the rifle because she could outshoot Barry every time and they both knew it—he was from Buffalo, New York and hadn't held a gun before Basic Training.

The CSAR bird had climbed and its guns were hammering down at something she couldn't see. But it was coming their way fast. The occasional explosion on the ground didn't stop whatever was on the move in their direction. All of the other helos were busy to the west, this end of the battle was up to the lone CSAR Black Hawk.

Noreen had seen more than enough firefights from the ground. And she knew The Jar's firing pattern well enough to pick it out anywhere. She should give the guy a break—he was damned good.

Xavier Jones was better.

He used a Minigun the way she used a surgical knife, with precision and speed. Operating theaters always made her a little crazy to watch—the surgeons moved so damn slowly. If she had an artery to clamp off to save someone's life, she sliced deep and got there as fast as she could. Battlefield surgery wasn't pretty, but it had to be effective.

In comparison, Mason waved a broadsword of bullets and Xavier used a rapier—fast, precise, and (she hoped for her sake) lethal.

Still, the helo was moving closer as they dodged and weaved above whoever was on the ground.

A line of pickups rolled into view. The second one exploded, scattering metal and bodies in all directions.

Ignoring the carnage, she lined up on the first vehicle. The Ranger's first round took out the windshield a moment before her shot took out the driver—half a second change and it would have been the Ranger's kill and not hers. Through the scope she could see the front passenger grab for the wheel, but it was too late—they caught a big rock and it rolled the truck up and over.

Killed by a woman—they weren't going to heaven.

How much that must gall them when they found out after crossing over. She had few doubts that the admitting room to the afterlife was taking full retribution on *all* of ISIS, but she did like adding that extra mark to their eternal damnation.

The battle blurred.

Some fighters who were thrown clear from the destruction gathered up their rifles. She, Barry, and the Ranger picked off the ones they could.

Another truck squeezed by the flipped one. Xavier killed that one while The Jar took out the next in line.

During a brief lull, someone shouted "Now!" over the radio.

Between one eye blink and the next, the Black Hawk was hovering two steps away with its belly touching the rocks.

Xavier reached down to help and the two Rangers were whisked aboard. Barry climbed in and Noreen barely had a moment to grab her med bag before a massive hand clamped down on her vest and lifted her aboard one-handed.

Xavier's strength was a visceral shock—as if his grasp had an actual g-force to it.

He thumped her down on the deck, snapped a three-meter monkey line to her vest to keep her aboard, and was back in his seat faster than she could catch her breath.

As the helo peeled away, Xavier and Mason

wiped out the last of the line of new arrivals down below.

"One dead, one stable," she managed to call despite how breathless she felt.

Cruiser acknowledged her report and began to once more circle outside the battle zone just in case there were more wounded during the night's action. Barry was seeing to the Ranger with the screwed-up knee—she bagged his buddy.

When the battle finished with no more injuries, the big Chinook circled down to gather up the ground forces and the very few surviving assailants, now prisoners.

"You are one chill medic, Miss Guardian," Xavier's voice rumbled as they turned for home.

She didn't feel "chill," not with the memory of how it had felt to be lifted to safety by Xavier.

Chapter 3

*A **dozen missions in*** a dozen nights and Xavier decided that Noreen's nicknames were justified: Guardian of the Night, Angel of Death, Bitch of Black Death, and all of the others he began hearing from the rest of the team. Though in her favor, she was only a bitch when something came between her and the person she was rescuing.

Even when what they had was a wounded bad guy, she still became especially fierce. They didn't want her help, most of the extremist radicals would rather die than be touched by a woman. One time she'd pulled her sidearm and shoved it half into a guy's mouth to shut him up so that she and Barry could stitch him back together. He'd kept yammering around the barrel until Xavier had taken the gun and flipped off the safety—then the guy had shut up and let her work.

Female Night Stalkers were still few and far between—despite being the only Special Operations team to actively recruit women before it was mandated by law—but there was no questioning that Noreen deserved to be one. He'd flown CSAR for years, but never seen anyone like her.

He asked around about the survival rate of her patients and came away surprised that she wasn't nicknamed "The Savior" no matter how sacrilegious it might be. That dead Ranger the first night was a complete exception once Noreen Wallace got her hands on them.

The other problem he was having was that she was an officer and he was enlisted.

Since not thinking about Noreen Wallace wasn't working for him, he'd shifted to a tactic of avoidance on the ground. She was still right there, so close and alive on every mission, but he made sure he was long gone before she'd restocked the helo's med gear.

However, Balad Air Base didn't offer the level of evasive options it once had. Gone were the days of forty thousand US personnel. Now Balad was manned by two very distinct groups that didn't come together. The main contingent was a few thousand members of the Iraqi Air Force and their F-16s. The other was the Americans: a single Night Stalker company, the Special Operations Forces they were responsible for delivering and rescuing, and a small collection of support personnel. Total count closer to one hundred than two.

His first tour had been here at "The Big Snake" of Camp Anaconda. Now back to its original Balad Air Base name, it was almost unrecognizable. The "downtown" with Subway, Burger King, and all the other food joints were gone. The outdoor Olympic-sized swimming pool had a nasty green tinge to the water, the indoor one was bone dry. And the first-run movie house was now third-run Iraqi propaganda films—when it was running at all. Most of the housing was a ghost town—so bad that they'd even been advised to avoid the southeast quadrant of the base for security reasons.

Dropping from forty thousand to less than two hadn't built a lot of community spirit. He'd been to FOBs—Forward Operating Bases—that were little more than HESCO barriers and machine gun mounts that were cheerier.

For something to do, the Night Stalker enlisteds had taken over an old briefing room, scrounged up a few pinball machines from various places, and installed a soda and munchies fridge. Various chairs and couches and a big screen TV for video games had made it about as welcoming as the inside of a Black Hawk after a battle. Maybe after a battle and a dust storm just before it was hit by a hurricane. But it was still an okay place to hang.

Tonight had been quiet, a short mission (back before midnight) and no casualties. To avoid the

Wreck Room, as they'd dubbed it, he'd spent a couple hours out on the range. Mason (Noreen had let him off the The Jar hook but hadn't replaced it with anything else yet) came out with him and they'd run through a couple hundred rounds apiece.

That first night he never should have missed the first shooter and the master sergeant helped him figure out why. It was Mason who spotted it. Without realizing it, Xavier had typically flown on the left side of the Black Hawks throughout his career, letting him steady his right shoulder (his shooting shoulder) against the back of the copilot's seat. Now he was sitting right side and it felt twisted.

They rigged up an old car seat that had been dumped nearby, with no sign of what had happened to the car itself, against a side wall that simulated the cramped position of the gunner's seats. He worked at it until he had a better feel for the shift. Back and forth, back and forth—they'd taken turns switching the seat side to side, again and again, until they were both shooting evenly no matter their position. Then they'd shot another stack of clips apiece to anchor it into muscle memory. If he and Mason had been scoring—which they both said they weren't but clearly were—they'd have tied. He could get to like Mason.

The master sergeant headed to dinner— which in a Night Stalkers clock-flipped world of nighttime missions and daytime slumber was about

0300—while Xavier visited the quartermaster to sign off for the spent rounds.

When he came back out, there she was outside the office—and up in the air.

Noreen had shed her Kevlar for an Army-tan t-shirt and it clung to her in all the best ways. She perched atop a twelve-foot concrete T-wall barrier as if sitting on the narrow top of the inverted *T* shape was the most natural place for her to be. Her position might be Humpty-Dumpty, but her grin was pure Cheshire Cat.

"Looking pretty damned pleased with yourself, Cap'n Luc." Guess he was grinning too.

"Feeling pretty damned pleased, Miss Alice."

She laughed at his reference to *Alice in Wonderland,* then with alarming lack of care, she pushed off the wall. A foot planted on the slope of the wide base changed her vertical fall into horizontal motion. He expected a dive into the dirt with a roll—instead she hit with both feet, took the landing shock all into her knees, then punched her excess momentum into a no-hand, mid-air somersault, coming to a standing stop not two feet from him.

"Having fun impressing the shit out of me?" She was so close that he could smell her, could feel her heat despite the warmth of the summer night.

"Always."

"You're giving me trouble, Guardian."

"And why is that, Cap'n?"

"Your color."

* * *

Noreen hammered a fist into his solar plexus—it hurt like punching the T-wall behind her.

Xavier did little more than grunt.

She went to storm off but Xavier grabbed her wrist. He caught her other fist while it was still in mid-flight at his jaw, clamping his hand over hers like a massive cargo net over a lone chicken from her family's farm—it suddenly wasn't going anywhere.

"Whoa! That came out wrong." He still wasn't letting her go.

"You're one of those bastards who only dates white women. As if my skin isn't good enough!" She couldn't believe that she'd fallen for that. For two weeks he'd been playing Mr. Good Guy and it turned out he was Mr. Major Asshole.

"I meant silver."

She stopped struggling against his iron grip and he let her go. He was even stronger than Big John and not half as friendly—her wrists hurt.

He held up his hands palm out as if to show he meant no harm. As if.

"Silver? I'm sure as hell not silver."

"Your metal is."

And she finally got it. Her first-lieutenant officer's insignia bar was silver, he was a four-striper, sewn-patch enlisted. Relationships were a no-go between enlisted and officers per Army regs. At least in most places. Her brother's company, 5th Battalion D Company, was a little odd on that. Her big brother had married Connie, both sergeants, and they'd continued to serve together in the same unit—unheard of. And John's first Night Stalker commander had married another, both majors.

But Connie's closest friend, Kee, was a sergeant who'd married a captain while still serving. It was okay now that they were out of the military—he was consulting on military matters at the very highest levels and Kee had finally joined the FBI's Hostage Rescue Team out of Quantico—but they hadn't been when they got married. *Really* unheard of.

"And, for the record," he glanced around, apparently making sure they hadn't attracted an audience from inside one of the supply offices, "you've got about the nicest skin this boy ever saw."

"I was *talking* to you, not offering to drag you off into some dark corner for sex."

"Oh," and he looked disappointed, sad puppy disappointed, which was actually cute on six-four of Night Stalker badass. "Sorry, my bad."

She was *not* thinking about sex with Xavier. *Really* not.

And there was no way she'd perched up there waiting for him. Nor was she impressed that he'd looked up. Most people were two dimensional beings, looking right, left, ahead, and—if well trained—back. He'd looked up, even though she'd been dead silent and perched above all except the faintest backwash of the security lights.

She had liked that about him.

Now she wanted to jump back atop her T-wall and run down the line. This stretch of them continued for half a kilometer, with only person-wide gaps through the base, for blast suppression of incoming mortars. There were wider gaps for vehicles, but those were kept to a minimum. During the US occupation, Balad had been nicknamed Mortaritaville for how often al-Qaeda had shelled them. Before ISIS had been driven out of the immediate area, they'd done the same, shelling the Iraqi Air Force elements that were now here.

Many of the barriers had been painted with unit insignia during the tenure of the Coalition Forces, now sun-faded.

"I…" he fumbled with his rifle for a moment. "Shit! Sorry, Noreen. You're about the most impressive lady I've met in or out of the service. Seriously sucks tamping down those fantasies. But you didn't ask for them."

She wanted to rub it in, but he looked seriously contrite. Besides, her own motivations were suspect and she *definitely* didn't want to go there.

However, hadn't he just confessed to having fantasies about her? They were probably guy-in-the-shower fantasies, but what if they were more than that?

Her own felt like more than that. Only now did she realize that he'd been avoiding her on the ground. Fun, smart, tough-as-hell on a mission— invisible on the ground. Which was why she'd finally hunted him down. Of all things, his *avoidance* had piqued her interest.

"Well," she sighed. "If you insist on being *completely* honest…"

"Not in the habit of it," but he didn't quite hold a straight face. "Seems like you're a bad influence. Of course, if *you* insist on being completely honest…" His handsome features went all the way to grin.

Was it so obvious on her own face that she'd been thinking about him? Her brother was gonna kick her ass if she fell for an Army grunt. She could just hear him, *You're better than that.* It didn't matter that he himself was an Army grunt and the best man she'd ever met.

Best man. Not a chance that Xavier fell into that category. He had bad-boy past written all over him. Actually, by the light of the security lamp she could see that some of that was literal—blue ink that barely showed against his dark skin. If a person with his skin color wanted a tat to show, they'd use white ink. But if it was just for him…

She reached out and traced a finger along the line of it, just above his wrists. Funny that she hadn't noticed it before. His skin seemed to shiver at her touch.

"What…" Noreen couldn't make them out.

"Broken shackles."

"You don't seem like one of those guys wrapped up in 'the black man's burden' thing."

Xavier huffed out a sigh. "Broken from *my* past."

"Before you were beamed into the Army."

"Yeah, something like that. How about you? Got any?"

"Tats? I hate needles. Why do you think I became a medic?"

That earned her the laugh she'd been after. Then she waited. Apparently he was willing to fantasize about her, but not talk to her about anything real like his precious past.

"Whatever." She took two steps, then ran straight at the wall. With a hard kick and a quick grab, she was back up on top of the barricade. She turned to walk away along the foot-wide tops when she heard a slap and grunt behind her.

Xavier didn't have the technique, but he'd gotten his fingers over the top edge. With his massive strength, he swung a foot up sideways and was seated astride the wall a moment later.

"Quite the view."

She couldn't read his voice without seeing his face. They were now above the main wash of the pathway lights. She glanced around. The barren, trampled dirt and battered one-story buildings of Balad Air Base stretched away in all directions except the airfield itself. Most of that view was blocked by the angular lines of tall sheet-metal hangers. The pathway lights were kept low so as not to aid mortarmen in their targeting if they started up again.

Here, atop the wall, they were in darkness. At night it felt both freeing and safe. They were as good as invisible but it let her see a wider vista that reminded her of home.

But she didn't need to read his expression to tell that he was looking directly at her. If she ran, even money said that he'd follow. This wasn't some ROTC freshman or first tour dude; Xavier was a Special Operations Aviation Regiment Night Stalker. A foot-wide path along the top of the T-walls wasn't going to stop him any more than the twelve-foot vertical height had.

She sighed and sat down cross-legged atop the next barrier in the line.

"You're beautiful," which was not the first thing she'd meant to say, even if he was. "But you don't talk to me, not really, so this is going nowhere."

* * *

Xavier rubbed his hand over his scalp and decided that he needed to shave tomorrow.

Beautiful. That was a new one on him. But if that's how Noreen wanted to tag him, he wasn't going to complain. He was also damn glad she telegraphed her punches or his gut would hurt even more than it still did.

"I was born in the Army—"

Noreen started to rise before he could finish his goddamn sentence. And there was no way he was going to be able to chase her through the air with the way she moved.

"Sit your fine ass down, girl. You wanta hear this shit or not? Your call. One time offer."

He could see her hesitate, then resettle like a sexy Buddha atop the wall. Her camo pants and dark skin were nearly invisible except for the occasional glint from her eyes. The buff-colored t-shirt showed up like a disembodied perfect torso. She wanted "beautiful"? Damned woman should look in a mirror.

"I was born in the Army because it's colorblind, or closest I've ever found. From Day One any boot dumb enough to make an issue of it went down hard. It was only a matter of whether it was me or the drill sergeant who got to him first. Rednecks don't stay that way long, at least on the outside, during Basic. Be nice to think the inside changes too, once they see they'd be dead if you weren't shooting right beside them. I liked that shit."

"And before?" Noreen's voice was soft as a nighttime desert breeze, and no longer quite so chilly.

"My parents were white—"

"Yeah. And mine were Chinese."

"You gonna let me finish a goddamn sentence here?"

Her t-shirt sketched a shrug in the darkness that said maybe yes and maybe no. His eyes were adapting enough that he could make out some of her face. He'd guess on the *maybe no* side of things.

"They were white *wannabes*. White jobs in white offices and a big house in the very best of the 'burbs. Private school with the white kids and a few other white wannabes. By the time I was twelve they were talking about Ivy League schools and all that shit. Maybe I was young and stupid, but none of that sounded like me. So I sought out 'my own kind' on the streets."

"Why was that stupid?"

"Because I trooped my sorry ass out to Prichard, of all ultimate pits. If you don't know it, it's a piece of Mobile that keeps winning 'Worst City in Alabama' awards. There I fell in with crackheads, petty thieves, carjackers, and a ton of other shitheads who wouldn't know an opportunity if it punched out their damned faces. But they were my color, my kin inside and out—or so I thought. How I didn't die or get caught by the system in those years beats the shit out of me."

"Maybe some angel was watching out for you, Captain Luc."

"Some angel like you?" Not a snowball's chance that was gonna happen in a hole like Prichard.

She shrugged. It was enough to make him smile.

"Wish you had, not that I'd have understood what you were at that point. I was a cocky bastard. My 'angel' turned out to be a big, ugly, black dude. I went into the Army Recruiter on an eighteenth-birthday dare to prove just how tough I was—way tougher than any mere soldier creep; that was a fact, Jack. Turned out I'd walked into an Army *Medical Brigade* Recruiter, shows you how much I knew. Black dude there was a seriously squared-away local. Begged to be assigned to Mobile when the post came open because he wanted to help. Made sure I wasn't out of his sight until a white buddy of his from Regular Army showed up—they'd served two tours together. You could see how goddamn close they were."

"But that isn't the day you were *born?*"

"No. It was stepping off the bus at Fort Benning. The Drill didn't give a good goddamn about my skin—he chewed me up and down just like everyone else there. Me, the six-foot-two of white pencil-neck geek, the Asian kid who coulda been rolled along he was so short and heavy—he went Green Beret in his third year if that don't beat all. Didn't matter to the drill sergeant. To him we were all squat until we'd proven ourselves. That's when I knew I'd done it right. Never forgot the Med recruiter though. I bucked for a slot as a CSAR crew chief the minute I heard there was such a thing."

"What about your parents?"

"Disowned my sorry ass at fourteen. Said they were done with me. Didn't want me tarnishing their reputation. Sent back my GED certificate when I got it. Doesn't matter if I put my rank and unit on the return address on the Christmas card I send every year. Comes back, 'Refused by Sender' as if that ain't some shit. Tried contacting them separately. No luck either side of the house."

"Assholes come in every color."

"That's the damn truth. Not saying I was some kinda joy as a kid, but they both got some serious issues. I get cards from those two recruiters sometimes, though. Real, handwritten ones. Couldn't believe it at first, but I do the same back to them whenever I find a good one." Too bad Balad sucked for cool cards. All of which was way too much shit about him. "You got a past, Guardian Angel?"

"Yep." Then she did one of those liquid moves and climbed to her feet like a gymnast on a balance beam—leaning over backwards, planting her hands behind her atop the wall, then kicked over through a handstand until she was once again on her feet a story in the air on a wall one foot wide.

It was the kind of move that grabbed him by the balls. Beauty, grace, and power all in one steaming hot lady.

"Come on." Rather than jumping down, she walked away from him along the top of the wall.

He eased up to his feet carefully, as any *normal* human would, and followed along the wall trying not to think about the long fall if he screwed up.

* * *

Noreen needed some space to think, but didn't want to leave Sergeant Xavier Jones behind either. She moved slowly along the top of the wall, not sure where she was going, but listening until she was sure he was following. He moved quietly for such a big man.

He was an orphan, or might as well be, which hurt her heart. However, that wasn't enough reason to do something stupid.

His answer to his awful parents had been to fight his way into the Night Stalkers, a height very few could climb. She knew. The pilots had a ninety percent wash-out and the rest of the crew weren't far behind. Like her big brother and Connie, she'd made it and she knew exactly what that meant.

And he wasn't some raring-to-go hothead with a Minigun—he'd asked for CSAR, a truly thankless job for a gunner. Those who flew to the front were always teasing CSAR fliers about not being up to the fight, until they needed a rescue. They were more respectful after that.

She hopped over a couple of four-foot gaps and kept moving. Glancing halfway back, she could see Xavier doing it with one long stride.

"Where you leading, Noreen?"

If he'd tagged her with any of the nicknames he kept trying on her, she'd have scoffed and kept moving. But her name stopped her. She didn't run away from things, not even at such a slow pace. She always faced her challenges.

Turning ninety degrees, she dropped down onto a picnic table, hopped to the ground, then shifted out of the way. Xavier followed by lowering himself by his hands and then dropping the last few feet to the ground.

"Where the hell are we?"

"It's the back patio of the old USO club." The wooden decking was heavily covered with sand. The couple of picnic tables and benches were equally dusted. The tight T-wall barrier made for a panoramic concrete view.

"Shit. I used to hang here back in the day. Looked just about as nice back then."

The back of the building was open and dark. One security light leaked through a narrow gap at a turn in the barrier wall, lighting the space in warm shadows. He looked magnificent in his camos and black t-shirt with his rifle still slung across his back.

"Why here?"

Noreen didn't know until she was already in motion.

* * *

She slid into his arms in a single smooth stride. He'd thought her delicate when he'd lifted her aboard the helo so easily on that first night. Then tough as nails when she'd punched him, and finally fragile for how small her wrists felt in his big clumsy hands after he'd blocked her punches.

All of that was right.

The woman who slid into his arms was slender, strong, and soft. And she had a kiss that started like the desert during a perfect sunset—warm but with a cool serenity—and a finish that made him feel battered by a whirlwind.

Xavier hadn't been saving himself for anybody, but if he had been, it would be for a woman who felt like Lieutenant Noreen Wallace.

Lieutenant.

He pulled his hands off her ass and put them on her waist to walk her back one step. She almost took one of his lips with her by a playful nip of her teeth.

"I know what you're going to say, Cap'n Luc. So don't waste time saying it."

"You a mind reader now, too?"

"Can't we just for one moment pretend that we're alone and all that doesn't matter," she waved a hand at the far side of the towering T-wall.

Against his own better judgment, his hands were pulling her back in. He hadn't moved away from the wall, and now she had him pinned to it.

It wasn't merely her fine form that was so overwhelming, nor the powerful muscles she'd built. She came at him with an enthusiasm he'd never experienced before in his life. It was as if all of that daily joy she spilled out of her during the long night missions came slamming into him in one mighty blow.

He held her, lifted her, and groaned as she clenched him tight.

She rubbed her hands over his bald head. "If you're growing it out for me, don't."

He definitely had to shave in the morning. He usually went three days between; for her he'd do it twice daily as long as she didn't stop doing what she was doing.

Her fine fingers were gentle yet possessive. Some women were put off by his bald-by-choice, some called it sexy. But no one had traced the shapes of his scalp the way Noreen did while she was kissing him.

He rolled over and pinned her back against the warm concrete wall. He leaned back enough above the hips so that he could investigate just how good she felt. Rather than going for her chest, he ended up tracing her jaw and her lips instead so that he could feel her smile as their lower bodies pressed hard together and shuddered with need.

Then she took his big hand in both of hers and kissed his palm. The sensation shot straight into his chest.

"Just in case."

"In case what?" he managed on a gasp.

"In case you ever need an extra smile," he could feel her lips curve against his palm.

Because of course Noreen would know exactly what he'd been doing.

Chapter 4

She didn't take him that night, it was too much too soon. Or the next, because the flight was long and the fight brutal. Besides, she was enjoying the zing every time they looked at each other or passed close enough to brush shoulders—at least her shoulder. He was so damn tall that she brushed him barely halfway up his arm.

But when two nights became two weeks, she wondered if she was losing her mind—or her touch. No man she was interested in avoided her for that long. Especially not ones who generated a crackle of energy between them brighter than the static sparking a bright circle off the tips of a helo's rotor blades in a dust storm. She no longer wanted Sergeant Xavier Jones; she needed him.

Noreen Wallace *never* needed a man. She liked

men—the right ones could be a serious amount of fun—but they always grew boring. She never stuck with a man past his expiration date. And she'd always found that date eventually—usually sooner rather than later. When she did, at least it was an excuse to buy another tight blouse or short mini-skirt just to make them whimper once they'd lost her. They also made her dad worry, while Mama just shook her head and laughed—both nice bonuses.

In the Army it was tougher. She'd collected fewer men, and the ending of relations was best kept on the QT for everybody's sake. Besides, all of her girl clothes were back home in Oklahoma. She'd also made a habit of only dating men of the same rank, but Xavier was long past tempting her.

"Tonight," she'd practically snarled at him as they trotted side by side from the night's mission briefing to the helo. "At the USO. Don't care when the flight is done."

"You know how much I'm gonna hate that," he grinned down at her.

"Not a bit?"

"Not even a tiny little one."

They'd stolen a kiss here, a cuddle there, and an exquisitely long yet painfully slow grope aboard the Black Hawk when they'd met there alone by chance to restock ammo and medical supplies.

They'd also spent a lot of time talking. Usually in public, over meals or during mission flights. Not about anything serious—too public for that—but still it felt real. It fast became clear that he was a seriously thoughtful guy. He talked about why he'd done eight years in CSAR, even drew Mason into the conversation. He didn't have her brother's gift of storytelling, but there was a brutal honesty to everything he said. As if he wasn't taking crap from anyone—least of all himself.

Thinking about what it was going to be like to make love with Xavier had her messing up the preflight supply check enough times for Barry to eye her strangely.

Xavier, on the other hand, appeared as calm as ever.

She was half tempted to torture him a bit when the time came, just to make him feel as she did. She knew she wouldn't though. At this point, she'd take him any way she could get him and he knew it, the smug bastard. Even his grin as they all closed doors, harnessed in, and headed aloft was just the normal-friendly look he gave her every time they went aloft. He even gave Barry a friendly "Hey!" that had her rolling her eyes.

What was *wrong* with her?

She never got this way about guys. Not back in ROTC, not while working her way up through the med corps, and not *ever*.

She leaned into the hard maneuvers hoping they'd jar her out of her mood.

That's what it was—just a mood.

Yeah, a mood that said she hadn't been laid in too long. She hadn't minded the last long dry spell, nobody had come along to bother breaking it for. It was the two weeks since they'd vaulted back over the walls of the USO together that had gone so far past reason.

Noreen looked at Xavier in profile in the red-lit darkness of the Black Hawk. His attention was where it was supposed to be, out the window and looking ahead.

So why was her attention entirely on how fast he could get into her camos?

There was no way she really *cared* about him.

Not a chance.

* * *

Xavier's blood pressure had left the planet within seconds of Noreen's invitation. She wasn't the sort of woman that you slammed up against a wall and pounded into, no matter how close he'd come to doing exactly that.

And there was a fear factor as well. If they were caught, he could be screwing up her career…and his. He'd been born in the Army, that had been his mantra for eight years now. His goal was to serve until he died—preferably of old age.

But the risk of Noreen's career was enough to have him holding back as hard as he could, even though he knew what he'd do given the least opportunity.

So he'd waited—waited for her to not want him the way he did want her since that first moment he'd seen her crossing the hangar. What he wasn't ready for was how it felt that she'd turned toward him rather than away.

He tried to remember the arrogant little asshole who had stormed out of his parents' home so long ago. And the teen who was so convinced that he was such hot shit back in Prichard, taking his first whore at fourteen. But he couldn't reconcile those two twerps with the guy who had a chance at a woman like Noreen Wallace.

So he kept his face just enough out the gunner's window for the cool desert air to brush away the flaming heat in his cheeks. His whole body felt turbocharged.

"Huh!" he grunted at the night as a fresh realization sank in. He'd *never* aspired to a woman like her. Maybe a piece of it was because he'd never met anyone quite like her. Or maybe he knew he'd never attract the notice of someone so spectacular.

Now that he had, it made him think a bit about the broader scope. What else had he taken for granted? Or, worse yet, rejected out of hand because it had been his parents' values? Maybe there was some good shit there among all of the guilt and manipulation crap.

What if—

The sudden slowing of the helo rocked him hard into the back of the pilot's seat, even rapped his helmet hard on the window's frame.

If they'd reached their holding station, that meant that the extraction was already in progress.

Tuned in now, he could hear that the Delta operators were already on the ground. A woman minister—bringing word to the heathens—and, god help him, a Japanese tourist had been swept up by the insurgents. Their executions were planned for the next day unless the Iraqi forces all quit and abandoned their jobs—like there was a chance in hell of that happening.

The transmissions were eerily silent as Delta infiltrated from their drop-off point—racing two kilometers over the night desert.

Over the radio there was a brief "Oh fuck," then a boom that was cut short—probably when the radio was destroyed along with its owner. Even from their hold distance, Xavier could see the brilliantly-lit plume of the IED's explosion flaring up into the night sky. For a moment, it lit the whole center of the small village. Then another bloomed upward and another, like hideous mushrooms of death. They were daisy-chained together to try and kill a whole team at once, with the trigger plate set out at the farthest point.

He and Noreen shouted, "Go!" in unison, but Vince was already racing them into the fray.

* * *

It was the ultimate nightmare scenario. The Air Mission Commander was telling them to hold shy of the compound even though she could see friendlies writhing in the dirt.

"Not safe to land. Not safe to walk. CSAR hold."

So they held and all she could do was impotently fume. If she went down and stepped on another trigger plate, she'd kill herself and maybe put a whole other section of the ground team at risk.

That didn't stop her from eyeing the Fast Rope—kick it out, slide down, it would be too late to stop her.

"Don't you be thinking 'bout what you're thinking about," Xavier's voice was a low grumble. It didn't come over the intercom into her helmet; instead, he'd switched himself out of the circuit so that only she would hear it. He hadn't even turned to her.

"How do you know what I'm thinking?" Her snarl went out over the intercom. *Damn it!*

Xavier gave a noncommittal shrug.

It sucked that he was right.

He continued scanning the ground, his gun aimed high and his attention aimed low.

She watched as the ground team dragged their casualties behind a low row of stones in a corner of the yard, some leaving long trails of blood in the dirt.

"Cleared to triage area only," the AMC announced. "Do not land."

She wouldn't think about how she was supposed to evacuate them if the helo couldn't land—slow winches didn't work well under enemy fire. That was a problem for some later moment.

Vince brought the CSAR bird in low.

She and Barry jumped to the ground and dropped to all fours. They stayed low as weapon's fire continued to spit against the compound's walls above their heads. Even kneeling could put them in harm's way—it wasn't all that much of a wall.

Only meters above them, Xavier answered with hard bursts from his Minigun. A shower of hot 7.62 mm brass tumbled out of the sky and rained down on them.

"Goddamn it, Vince," she shouted over the radio. "Don't need a hot metal shower down here." The Miniguns dumped overboard eighty rounds a second of hot, two-inch-long brass casings when they were firing.

The helo slewed sideways so that the brass was raining down a dozen feet to the side.

She could never remember if the second thing she did was see it or hear it…

No question about the first thing though, she *felt* it.

The blast lifted her up and sideways, slamming her into the compound wall on the far side of the prone casualties.

Her thought as she briefly flew above the people she was supposed to be treating was that this was going to be a bitch unless she could grow real angel wings—fast.

The outer wall of the compound was a heavy structure that stopped her cold. She hit flat on her back—spread-eagled sideways in the air. Her brief urge to create a snow angel on the wall was defeated as she dropped to the ground.

Everything hurt.

Her ears rang despite the buffering of the helmet. She was going to be black and blue from her helmet to her boots from that slam into the wall.

Her eyes…she hadn't been facing the blast so she could see everything just fine. The line of casualties had been below the blast. Barry lay prone over several of the bodies, but he was back off them in a moment showing that it had been a protective gesture and he wasn't part of the body count.

He was at her side in a second.

She could see his mouth moving, but there was only the ringing in her ears and the heavy beat of the helicopter not five meters above them.

It wavered.

She blinked hard, but still it wavered. It wasn't her vision, it was the Black Hawk. Five tons of airborne lethal wasn't supposed to waver.

The explosion had momentarily roiled the air and, without clean air, the rotor blades couldn't get enough lift. The Black Hawk slid sideways like a stumbling drunk—then clipped a blade on the roof of a house. That signed the helo's fate.

Noreen grabbed the lifting ring on the front of Barry's vest and pulled him down. He landed on her hard enough to hurt even more, but she couldn't look away from the helo. It tumbled out of the sky like the final flip of a dying catfish in the bottom of a boat.

Chunks of rotor blade flew in all directions.

The helo slammed down on one side.

The shredding rotors beat dust into the air until the Black Hawk disappeared behind a massive cloud that even her night vision couldn't penetrate.

The knee-high wall that hadn't been able to protect her from the blast shielded them this time as the last flung bits of composite blade spattered against the wall mere inches above them.

Suddenly everything was quiet—like the night had forgotten how to breathe. The Black Hawk's turbines whined down from scream to murmur to silence—someone was still at the controls.

She and Barry slowly turned to look. Miraculously, the helicopter was on its wheels, though it appeared to have done a full dog-in-the-dirt roll to get there.

It had ended up with its nose mostly facing her. She could see Vince was still shutting things down. Penny was at least moving beside him. But what about—

For the first time, fear slammed into her. It was unlike anything she'd ever experienced. Not her most extreme Parkour jump, not her first Fast Rope into an active battle, not the first time she'd been shot at for real.

It was visceral, acidic, pummeling terror—worse than the blast.

"Xavier." All she could manage was a croak.

Barry cautiously pushed off her and turned toward the downed helo.

* * *

Xavier tried to release his harness, but all raising his left arm did was make it hurt like hell—his arm didn't move one bit.

He couldn't reconstruct the last thirty seconds very well.

His Minigun mount was all twisted up. Jiggling the gun only left it aimed at a single point in the sky. He yanked at it one-handed, still his main weapon remained stubbornly aimed upward. It wasn't supposed to be possible to aim them upward, didn't want to be shooting out your own rotor.

Was that what had happened?

He leaned forward and looked up. No whirling disc. No rotor blades at all.

Straight ahead was a wall of unmortared sandstone blocks tall enough to block any view.

Compound. Right. They'd been inserting into a terrorist compound, delivering aid for a rescue gone wrong.

IED.

The weight of his falling brass should never have been enough pressure to trigger the mine—or every passing chicken would have blown itself up. It must have been partially triggered by that first blast that had ripped apart the ground team. His stream of spent brass had only finished the job.

"You just sitting there all day?" Mason. He was up and had his rifle in his hands.

"My ass *is* kinda comfortable here," Xavier kept it light. But trying again to reach his harness hurt like hell and it must have showed.

Xavier released it for him.

He turned to climb out of his seat, but his left arm didn't want to follow.

"Here," Mason took his wrist with surprising gentleness and tucked Xavier's left hand into a loop on his vest. "Feels like you dislocated your shoulder."

Xavier was a little surprised to discover that his right hand worked just fine. He must be more rattled than he'd thought. With his right hand, he freed his own rifle, then nodded for Mason to lead the way.

They dropped out of the helo and onto the ground at the same time Vince and Penny rolled out their doors.

"Four standing. Good sign," Vince limped heavily as he turned to survey his helicopter.

"Need to get a medic to look at that," Xavier's own words brought back the last image of the crash—Noreen flying through the air in the force of the blast.

"Noreen!" his voice roared out across the compound.

That's when he became aware of his immediate surroundings. There was still a full-on battle going down. The helicopter was mostly shielding them, but rains of gunfire crackled through the air. Chopped-off screams. Idiots shouting the name of their god as if He'd ever forgive them for what they were doing in His name.

Mason dropped to the ground and began firing at targets from beneath the helo. Penny dragged down Vince and they started doing the same.

Xavier ducked down and rushed toward the triage corner.

Barry was kneeling over a prone figure—one too small, even in full gear, to be a man.

Xavier cried her name again as he jumped over a gap in the chicken-high wall, then over the injured soldiers lying in the dirt. He couldn't raise his hand to stop himself and slammed his bad shoulder into the unforgiving rock of the high main wall. For a long moment all he saw was white sheets of pain.

The instant his vision cleared, he saw that Noreen was looking up at him.

But she wasn't getting up.

"What's wrong? Barry, you gotta fix her. How can I help? Shit, where are you hurt?"

* * *

Where was she hurt?

Her chest. Like her heart wanted to explode out of it.

Noreen had seen Xavier jump down out of the helo, rifle raised and ready in his hand like some mythic warrior.

She'd never seen a better sight in her life.

Then the very first thing he'd done? With bullets flying around him, while others had ducked for cover, huddling behind the safety of the helo?

Xavier had stood tall and roared out her name like a wounded beast. He'd sprinted through the hail of gunfire like it couldn't touch him. And it hadn't.

"I'm fine, I think." She had to shove at him to get him out of the way enough for her to sit up. Every muscle complained, but it didn't feel as if anything was broken. Instead it felt as if she'd sprained her entire body.

She was so glad to see him that she couldn't tolerate the feeling. It was too big and—

Her eyes landed on the injured that Barry was tending.

"Go!" She pushed again at Xavier, who was hovering over her as if she couldn't protect herself. "End this! I have work to do."

Xavier nodded once, then again.

"I'm fine."

At that he finally turned and hunkered down behind the low wall, resting his weapon on the top of it, and began firing. Like his tactics with the Minigun, he didn't just rip out a magazine. He fired one or two shots at a time and she'd bet that every one counted. His reloads looked strangely awkward, but she didn't have time to think about that.

She rolled to her knees to face the first patient and every muscle complained.

If this was "fine," she'd take a pass on being actually hurt.

Her armored vest had protected her shoulders and her helmet had made sure that she was only rattled rather than concussed or dead. Her ass had been less well defended and when she tried to sit on her heels, the pain was enough to make her vision blur for a moment.

"So don't sit on your heels," she told herself.

The wounded soldier looked up at her strangely. He was holding a blood-soaked compress to one arm with a hand from the other. That meant Barry was on triage and she was on treatment.

Noreen introduced herself.

When the soldier didn't answer right away, she pulled out a penlight to check his eyes for shock. Then he whispered, "The Angel of Death." Surprise, not shock.

"At your service," a quick once-over revealed no other obvious wounds and no pool of blood in the dirt beneath him. She began bandaging his arm and kept him talking. Like with so many of the guys she treated, it was mostly a one-sided conversation, but he responded enough to show he was okay.

When she had the bleeding stopped and the arm in a sling—three bullets had broken the bone, but no artery—he grabbed the load-out D-ring at the center of her armored vest with his good hand.

Some didn't want her to leave them because they were afraid of death in that moment. Some thought that because she patched them up, their future was destined.

"Thanks," was all he said before he let her go.

And people asked why she loved this job.

Chapter 5

Xavier lay back against the sloped rear hatch of a Chinook MH-47G helicopter. The cargo bay was crammed with forty-five Special Operations soldiers as well as the six people from his Black Hawk. The Chinook was such a beast that in addition to all the personnel, it had latched a couple of hundred-foot cables onto their downed bird and was bringing home the wounded machine as well as the warriors.

He watched Noreen and Barry as they worked through the crowd. The cargo bay was six-six high (in boots and helmet, he was always banging the ceiling), eight wide and thirty long. In a Black Hawk, there was only four-six and that he always remembered to duck for.

Half of the soldiers were slouched in the

fold-down jump seats along either side. Some chatting about the battle or girlfriends, some crashed into a nap because that's what you did on a flight. The rest were sprawled on the main deck. Most were sitting on their packs so that the truly injured could lie down in the crowded space.

No corpses though, at least no American ones.

Even though the hostages had been rescued in the first ten minutes and stashed in a corner of the triage area, the battle had raged for over an hour up and down the length of the village before they could arrange a clean extraction.

Vince had sprained an ankle during the rollover but was otherwise okay. The four of them had stood guard duty over the medical team, the hostages, and the attractive target of the downed Black Hawk. Mason had managed to resurrect his own Minigun—after that, keeping the area defended at least to one side had been much easier.

Aboard the Chinook with the rear ramp closed, the ramp gunner had nothing to do. So he too leaned back against the inclined ramp. Shooting the shit with him about the differences between Mobile and the Cleveland suburb where Ray had grown up helped pass the time and distracted Xavier from his shoulder.

That and watching Noreen. As he watched her, he noticed that she wasn't moving in her normal style. Every motion was considered. Rising when she'd been squatting over someone for any length of time was a slow process.

By the time Noreen reached the back of the helo, Ray the gunner had clearly decided that the conversation was too one-sided and he'd fallen asleep.

"Hey, Guardian."

"Hey, beautiful," she responded as she knelt down beside him.

"Still gonna take some getting used to that." But if that's what she wanted to call him, he wasn't going to complain.

She looked ready to collapse into the narrow space on his left. Ray was snoring quietly to his right.

He tried to raise his arm so that she could tuck in against his shoulder, but it caused him to hiss with pain. For a moment he'd forgotten about it.

"What's with you?"

"Mason thinks I dislocated my left shoulder during the crash," he shrugged, then wished to hell he hadn't done that either.

"Mason?" But she was already in action— poking, prodding, testing.

"Easy there," the warning was instinctive even though she was actually causing little pain. Her fine hands moved in a choreographed dance as she whipped out a triangular bandage and fashioned him a sling. She eased it on so smoothly that he barely felt anything. In moments, his pain had eased because the arm was better supported.

"Do you want a shot for the pain?"

"Nah, I'm good," he shrugged again. Shit, he had to stop doing that.

"It'll need an x-ray to make sure nothing's broken before a doc can reset it."

Xavier slid to the left, opening a space between himself and the ramp gunner. He held out his right arm and Noreen slid into it, laying her head on his shoulder. Still bulked up in their armored vests, it was awkward, but it was worth it.

"I should have checked on you sooner."

"You were taking care of guys who needed it. This sucks, but that's all. Though, I'm guessing tonight is out of the question?"

"Tonight?"

"The USO." Their planned tryst. He'd been looking forward to that all night. He rested his cheek on her hair.

"You touch my ass and I'd have to kill you."

"What? Why?"

"Point of first impact with that damned wall."

He tried to sit up to look at her, but between one arm in a sling and her lying on his other side, that wasn't happening.

"Nothing broken. But I'm not going to be sitting down for a week."

That explained why she'd been moving slower and slower. Blown up, rattled, hurting—and Noreen Wallace had done her job. He didn't know what else he expected. He'd already known that she was incredible, but now he had even more proof.

In moments she was asleep in his arms.

* * *

Noreen had woken up in a lot of strange places, but lying in Xavier's arms was both the least and the most strange.

It felt so right, so good. She knew he was asleep and it didn't matter. Her hand was resting on a stack of spent thirty-round magazines and his fingers were hooked behind the Velcro strap of her vest's shoulder closure. It didn't matter—it was such a good place to be.

Then she opened her eyes and realized that they were curled up together at the back of an overloaded Chinook. Fifty soldiers and fliers had seen them, watched them.

She never did this kind of thing in public. Never showed favoritism, even on the very few occasions when she had some. It was her job to treat these men and—never mind the regs—now they'd look at her like…like…like she was a woman, not a soldier.

Or that she was easy—or available. She'd consciously chosen her role as a female in the male-dominated Special Ops military. She wasn't the Slut or the Little Sister, she was the Warrior Princess. She'd studied the archetypes in college writing class and decided that the best way to take on the men was to become, in a way, their queen. That's why all of the nicknames didn't bother her, for who was more powerful than The Guardian of the Night or The Angel of Death?

Now, in one lapse of judgement, she'd flaunted

her X-chromosome and now she'd become a *girl*. All that effort spent trying to fit in—wasted!

She tried to push upright, but even in sleep Xavier held her tightly. When he woke enough to free her, she sat up—

And regretted it instantly. What had been merely stiff and sore had solidified into aching concrete. And the act of sitting made her wonder if she actually had broken her butt. It hurt like hell.

She managed to make it to her knees as Xavier fell back asleep.

Warrior Princess? Hell no. Not even *girl*. She'd traded them all in on Old Crone. She hobbled among the men, checking on the injured one by one. She changed out an empty saline bag, peeked under a dressing, pumped in some more painkillers to the worst hit, and continued about her duties. When she reached the front of the Chinook, Barry woke up and shuffled aside to make a space for her.

Even shedding her vest and sitting on it for padding didn't help much, but she sat.

"You okay, Noreen?" He kept his voice down to a whisper.

"Just a bit battered. Nothing that won't heal."

"Not what I'm asking about and you know it. Known you three years. Never seen you do that," he didn't even bother nodding toward the back of the helo.

Noreen looked down the length of the dimly lit cargo bay. Someone had turned down the lights for the couple-hour flight back to base.

Xavier Jones dominated everyone else. His big frame looked even bigger when she remembered how he'd rushed to protect her. Even more so now that she understood he'd been injured himself when he did so.

For a woman who never needed a protector—after all, she was a Guardian Angel by trade—she'd found a very unlikely one.

"I think I'm okay," she told Barry. "I'll let you know."

Because for the first time in her life, she wasn't sure herself.

* * *

Never, ever, tell a doc to just do it!

Xavier beat that lesson into his brain. Next time he had a shoulder reset he was gonna take the damn painkillers. Hell, just knock him the hell out.

It'll hurt, but only for a moment. Then the doc had braced himself like a football player on the front line and even that hadn't clued Xavier in.

Just do it!

Shithead.

But that didn't hurt half of what came next.

"Two weeks leave?" Xavier couldn't have heard the unit commander right. "You only grounded Vince for two days."

"His was just a sprain. Besides, that's what the doc said."

"What am I supposed to do with two weeks?"

"I'm not your granny. Just keep the damn sling on for four more days and get the hell off my base."

And now Xavier was standing in the hangar watching his crew saddle up without him. The maintenance techs had kicked ass through the day, replacing rotor blades, crumpled sheet metal, and his damaged gun mount. The Black Hawk was going to be flying sooner than he was.

Xavier had only been aboard for two weeks and this was *not* how he wanted to be remembered—injured and out. You couldn't trust a guy to not do the same next time. In clean for six months or a year, guys wouldn't think anything of you missing some action. But two weeks in, then two weeks out—when he came back they'd just be waiting for his next "excuse."

"Shit!"

"I know! It completely sucks!" Noreen said from close beside him. Until that moment, he hadn't noticed that the second medic wasn't her. Barry and some new guy were trotting out to the helo for tonight's mission.

"What are you doing here?"

"Grounded. Same as you. Seems I actually broke my tailbone when I hit the wall."

"How can you be a guardian angel with a broken tail? Doesn't it making flying tricky?"

"I sure could have used wings that last time I went flying. Doc agrees with you, no flying without an intact tailbone. Where are you going?"

Xavier shrugged with one shoulder; he was

getting better at remembering to do that. "Off base is what they're telling me. Kicking around Europe one-handed doesn't sound like much fun. How about you?"

"Home." She said it flat out with no hesitation. Simple fact.

So much for seeing if she'd hit Europe with him.

"Want to come?"

At first her suddenly soft words didn't make sense. Did he want to go home? His only home was Joint Base Lewis-McChord in Washington State—literally half a world away. Except he had nothing there other than an old car and some clothes. The barracks would be empty because his entire company was right here in Balad, Iraq.

Come home. Not *go* home.

That was a whole different kinda option.

He looked down at her, but Noreen was watching the helo winding up. It sprayed hot air and dust in their direction. It was making her eyes tear up, but she wasn't looking away.

She watched it hover, then climb aloft. Seconds later it disappeared into the darkness, trailing precisely five minutes behind the main flight. Then she turned those longing eyes on him.

No way could he say no to that.

Chapter 6

Their reception was way better than Noreen could have hoped. They found a cargo flight to the Night Stalkers' main base at Fort Campbell, Kentucky. The last four hundred miles to home was always a pain, but her brother kept a car on base for exactly that reason.

But when she went hunting for her brother's car, she found him instead. He was in the back corner of a massively cluttered hangar working on a Little Bird helicopter. There were four Black Hawks in different states of perfectly ordered disassembly. Three simultaneous overhauls by the look of, but with gear she didn't recognize. She was enough her brother's little sister to see that something different was being mounted on each one, but to what purpose she had no idea.

"John!" She squealed and threw herself at him.

"Nori!" He dropped tools that rang like happy bells when they hit the concrete, caught her, and gave her a bear hug that hurt like hell but was so totally worth it.

Her back may have been protected by the armored vest, but she'd still hit hard and every muscle complained. Plus her broken butt.

"What are you doing Stateside?"

"What about you?"

"I asked first."

"I asked second," she shot right back.

He laughed that big laugh she loved so much and hugged her again.

This time she couldn't cover her groan.

"What's up, Nori?" He was so strong that he held her up in the air to look at her like she was a little girl still.

"Bunged myself up."

Suddenly she was on her feet and John was inspecting her carefully.

"Nothing broken but my tailbone," she held up the stupid doughnut pillow she'd been sitting on for the long flight Stateside. "Pretty much pulled every single muscle in my body. Tip for the future: don't get yourself blown up."

He stopped fussing, then retrieved his tools and dropped them on a cluttered service cart before answering her. "Yeah, it sucks."

Then he looked up over her head and she could see the shift. In that instant her favorite brother, Big John, went away and First Sergeant John Wallace towered in his place.

"John, this is Xavier. He's a gunner on my helo. Got bunged up in the same explosion I did. He—"

And then she spotted her sister-in-law Connie.

Noreen raced over to her as she stepped down from a Black Hawk. Connie's hug was as gentle as the woman herself, but Noreen held it like she was never letting go. She actually had to sniffle to keep the tears at bay. She might be over a decade younger than her other three siblings, John, Janice, and then Larry—all with just a year between them. But John and Larry had still felt like brothers. Janice, however, despite being a year younger than John, had always acted more like an aunt that a sister. *That girl was* born *all grown up*, Mama Bee had always said.

The day John brought home Connie was the day she'd gotten a true sister.

Connie sniffled too.

Which made them both laugh. And that started the tears, at least on her side—Connie never cried. Noreen didn't know where the tears were coming from, but since she was with Connie, it must be okay.

"I'm so glad you're here." It wasn't clear who said it first and it didn't matter one bit.

* * *

Looking at the two women together was actually more uncomfortable than the big guy glaring at him. Xavier had never been that close to anyone. Couldn't imagine what it must feel like.

Connie was kind of a surprise. Noreen had talked a lot about her brother John and his wife, but never actually said anything about how they looked. John was Xavier's height and build, and his skin was closer to Xavier's darkness than Noreen's. Connie was even shorter than Noreen, light brown hair, and Caucasian—the seriously cute white girl next door. He'd pictured Connie as some perfect black woman, long and lean the way Noreen was. Instead she was short, nicely curvy, and very white. He was being slow to adjust his mental image.

Of course he had other problems at the moment.

Five-six of little white chick wasn't the issue. Six-four of pissed off older brother definitely was.

"Xavier." The guy said it like a statement and meant it like a hundred questions: the biggest one being *Tell me why I shouldn't beat your ass?* And he was one of the few people Xavier had ever met that just might be able to pull it off, even if Xavier didn't have one arm in a sling.

"Yes, sir," but he knew it was a mistake as soon as he said it.

John didn't even bother with: *I'm not a sir, I work for a living.* He just leveled a scowl at Xavier that threatened to melt the flesh from his bones. *This* was Noreen's beloved, gentle big brother that she couldn't stop telling stories about?

"Noreen was nice enough to invite me along when I had nowhere else to go."

"Nowhere else to go? Like some damned lost kitten?"

"No," Noreen came up on Xavier's sling side—which was good or otherwise he might have reached for her without thinking and that would have been bad. "Not like some *damned lost kitten.* He doesn't have a family. Well, he does, but they sound like complete shits."

"No family?" For some reason that stopped the big man in his tracks.

"None worth speaking about," Xavier managed to swallow the "sir," but just barely. Sergeant John Wallace was just that impressive.

Connie slipped up alongside her husband and his arm slid protectively around her shoulders. Strangest looking couple he'd ever seen, but they fit together anyway.

He'd labeled her "little white chick" dismissively in his thoughts, but he saw that was wrong. She didn't look pissed like Noreen's brother. Instead she inspected him carefully as if she already knew more about him than Xavier himself did. Suddenly he wondered which of the two was more dangerous: the big angry dude or the small quiet woman.

"So, we're both on med leave for a couple weeks," Noreen thankfully picked up the slack in her cheerful way as if nothing awkward was going on. "I wanted to go home. Can we borrow your car?"

"No," John grumbled out.

Xavier came up on his toes. Was he going to have to have it out with this dude here and now? John could mess with Xavier, but he wasn't going to let him take it out on Noreen.

"But if you wait a few hours, we can fly you home in that," John hooked a thumb at the Little Bird he'd been working on.

* * *

"How?" Noreen waved her hand around to indicate the Little Bird helicopter they were sitting in. She and Connie were in the backseat, because there was no way either John or Xavier would fit back here. They switched both of their headsets to an isolated circuit so that they could chat.

She felt like she should be refereeing for Xavier and John, but they were both big boys and would just have to figure it out at some point. Better here in the air than on the ground. She'd never seen anyone actually loom over her brother before, but Xavier definitely had. Her Warrior-Defender-in-a-sling. So damn cute she could melt.

Her stupid tailbone pillow made her several inches taller than Connie and she didn't like it. It felt all out of whack, but there wasn't anything she could do about it.

"John and I have been reassigned from active duty to the Headquarters and Headquarters Company. We're working on the next round of enhancements to the aircraft."

Which made perfect sense. SOAR's top two mechanics were already responsible for most of the innovations in the Night Stalker's customized airframes.

"One of the bonuses they dangled was that we can use a helo to go home on the weekends—it cuts the travel time to just over two hours. Usually we do in-flight testing en route, but sometimes we just fly."

"But why go to the HHC now? I thought you liked the field."

"We do. There's no better way to see how an aircraft performs than under actual battle conditions." But then Connie rested a hand on her belly and her rare smile showed up warm and soft.

"Oh my god!" Noreen knew right away. "I'm going to be an auntie!"

She wrapped her arms around Connie. Noreen had only delivered one or two babies over the years, but she'd studied plenty and they talked about nothing else for the first hour of the flight.

* * *

Xavier could feel the rotor's beat pulsing against him during the long, silent flight. It was broken with only the most stilted of conversation through the western part of Tennessee.

"Army." Big John broke the silence with another of his one-word statement-questions as they crossed the Mississippi River and entered the airspace over the southern tip of Missouri.

"Three tours before SOAR. Just made FMQ." John would know that Fully Mission Qualified for the 160th meant two more years of training hell on top of his six years of prior service.

"Gunner."

"Since the first day."

"Why CSAR?"

"Wow! Two words. You must be warming up to me."

"Don't push your luck."

Xavier decided that was good advice, especially with John at the controls of the racing helo and Xavier having no knowledge about how to fly one. He told the story of walking into the wrong Army recruiter's office on a dare.

That earned him a thoughtful grunt. Oh, right. He hadn't gone CSAR to target Noreen.

"She isn't some goddamned perk. I'm not a total shit. She's an amazing woman." Xavier confirmed that he got John's point.

"Damn straight."

That saw them out of Missouri and well over Arkansas, past the muddy farmlands and over the forests of the low rolling hills.

"Family."

"Like I said, nothing worth mentioning." Not a chance Xavier was going to be spilling about his sucky past to this guy.

Again the grunt and another fifty miles of silence.

Xavier wasn't going to be helping him none.

"You and she—" But her brother didn't seem able to finish the sentence.

It was the first time Xavier saw past the battle shield John had raised. John grimaced, like the question hurt him. Like…

Xavier almost laughed. He finally got what was going on. The guy wasn't being an asshole. He was being protective of his little sister. Xavier had no idea what that would be like. But if he'd had a little sister and she'd brought home some guy, he'd—

No. If she'd brought home some guy—that she was *screwing*—he'd have a goddamn coronary.

"No." He and she weren't.

And John relaxed the most since the first moment they'd met.

"Not yet," Xavier couldn't leave it alone.

John groaned. "Did *not* need to hear that."

"Better deal with it. 'Cause we sure as hell are going to. Soon."

"What's stopped you?"

Xavier raised his slinged arm, then winced and used his other hand to ease it back down into position.

"You invite yourself along?" He actually put a question mark on it this time.

"No. She invited me. Surprised the shit outta me."

"Uh-huh," John's look softened further. "I did the same to Connie. She's an Army orphan. Nowhere to go at all. Family fell in love with her on Day One. Except Nori. Nori barely let Connie in the door. Still don't know what changed her mind about Connie. I'm thinking hypnosis or something. Two are thicker than thieves ever since. There's all kinds of things Nori knows about my wife that I don't."

"Huh." Somehow he'd never thought that pretty little white chicks had ugly pasts. His parents might not be speaking to him, but it would be weird if they weren't there in their happy little suburb. Like he'd somehow belong even less than he did.

Big John had eased down in size. Somehow he looked more normal-sized as he flew the helicopter. He didn't have the ease of a trained Night Stalker pilot, but he was better than the average mechanic. To hear Noreen tell it, John and Connie were the top two mechanics in all of SOAR. That was saying a whole lot.

Xavier knew he was damn good himself—the unmentionable years working in a chop shop had paid off in bucking for a crew chief slot. Now he was going to have to scramble to keep up with John.

"Did you bring Connie home out of pity?" Xavier didn't know where the question had come from. He'd said yes to Noreen's invitation because he'd wanted to make love to her so badly. Was that why she'd asked him home? A good fuck? Or a pity fuck? Or… He didn't want to think about what was worse than that.

"No," John grumbled at him. "Maybe a little bit of feeling sorry for her. But that didn't even last for the length of the flight. I brought her to my family's home because I couldn't stop thinking about her."

Xavier grunted out his own acknowledgement. Whatever else, he certainly couldn't stop thinking about Noreen Wallace.

* * *

"So?" Connie's one-word question threw Noreen for a loop.

They'd covered everything starting from the fact that Connie and John had switched to the HHC only *in hopes* of having a kid. Even John didn't yet know that it had worked, so Noreen happily crossed her heart to promise secrecy—on the sole condition that Connie told him in front of the whole family so that she could be there to watch. And to heckle, though she hadn't mentioned that part of her plan out loud.

"That's why I didn't tell him when I found out two days ago. It should be with the family."

But she didn't know how to answer Connie's question. Didn't understand the answer herself.

"He's the new gunner on my helo."

Connie just nodded.

"He's…different."

"It's not because he's like your brother?"

Noreen had to laugh. "Xavier Jones is many things. Being like John in anything other than physical size isn't one of them. He's rude, rough, abrupt—"

"And you care about him a great deal."

"And I care about him a great deal," she sighed. She told the story of how he'd screamed out her name and rushed to her side in the middle of a battle as if she was the most important thing in the world.

Connie nodded. "I was trying to disarm… well, that's classified info even from you. But John was right there. I thought I loved him by then. But I didn't understand. The real moment was when he nodded for me to make the guess on how to do it. It wasn't just that he trusted me, but it was also that even if he could have gotten out of the possible blast radius, he wouldn't leave as long as I was inside it."

Noreen could only sigh.

It was *exactly* that feeling.

"Oh shit!"

And Connie's smile went radiant.

"No way!" But Noreen's protest sounded lame even to her own ears.

There was no way she loved Xavier Jones. It was way too soon for that.

She'd just brought him home for a vacation.

Just brought him home to meet…the most important people in her life.

Because she…

Oh shit!

Chapter 7

Xavier had never seen anything like what lay below the helo as they came in for a landing. Arkansas rolling hills covered in thick green trees had given way to flat farmland when they crossed into Oklahoma. Everything was so far apart that he found it hard to imagine. No walking from house to house out in this country.

John pointed out feed corn, wheat, and soybean fields as if you could actually tell such things from the air.

"See the gold. We've got grain sorghum in this year. That's a premium cattle feed. The brownish are is wheat." After crossing the Arkansas River, John appeared to have decided he was okay and was filling him in on the local scenery—which was all crops.

Which was nice of him, but under the lowering sun it all looked pretty much the same color of brown to him.

Xavier had grown up in a city and flown ever since. One thing about thirty-million-dollar helicopters, they always returned to base at night. Whether training at Joint Base Lewis-McChord in Washington state or kicking ass in Iraq, the only time he saw the countryside was from the air.

The Wallace's farm was a massive spread defined by the two different crop colors. There was a long barn with a line of garage doors. Even as they approached, a big tractor was heading into one of the bays—he wouldn't even try to guess at the purpose of the equipment it was dragging.

A big garden patch, probably vegetables, but also a whole section lush with flowers wrapped around a farmhouse that looked small from the air. It didn't look much bigger as John settled the helo into the side yard.

Before the engine was even shut down, people were coming out to glance their way and wave. A couple of guys from the garage shed. A woman on the house porch.

And then Noreen stepped down just as the rotors stopped turning.

It was like someone had hit the magic-family-moment switch.

There were cries of joy, which brought out more people. They rushed over and Noreen disappeared inside a sea of hugs. Parent-aged and brother-aged men piled right in with the women. A couple of little kids wormed their way in to embrace her knees.

Xavier had never seen anything like it. He braced himself for another round of pissed-off-big-brother type reaction when he himself finally stepped down. And was confused when even that simple thing didn't play out as expected.

"Hey, I'm Larry," a guy who was clearly John's slightly-shorter brother shook his hand like a long-lost friend.

Then he blinked hard and looked around without releasing Xavier's hand.

"Holy shit! Noreen brought home a guy." Larry's smile grew huge. "You must really be something. She's never done that."

Before Xavier could process that, an older, calmer version of Noreen gave him a light hug. "Welcome to the family."

Betsy—but call me Mama Bee because everyone else does—was more cautious, but still more polite than his own parents had ever been to anyone. No. Actually, his parents were perfectly polite—big-time emphasis on *perfect*—Mama Bee was honest and that meant so much more.

As the jostling and greetings settled down, Xavier ended up on the outside edge of the crowd. A man came up and introduced himself.

"I'm Noreen's father. My name is Paul, but you better just start off with Paps." His handshake and smile appeared genuine.

"How—" But Xavier couldn't figure out how to articulate it.

"How what?"

Xavier waved a hand at all of the people who had greeted him so warmly. Paps seemed to catch his meaning. He slapped Xavier on the shoulder, the good one mercifully.

"So you know Noreen, but you don't *know* her yet. My youngest is a force of nature. She sets her mind on something and all of us know better than to say a word. Not because we aren't thinking them, but because she loves proving us wrong after we've said them. She brought you home, that speaks a whole world of things."

Xavier considered asking what kind of things, then thought better of it.

Paps looked over at his daughter, who was talking a mile a minute with her mom and some woman he couldn't recall the relationship of, as they all headed toward the house. It was easy to see the joy he took in her.

"Son," Paps glad-handed his shoulder again. "You're in for a hell of a ride. Want some advice?"

Xavier shrugged a yes because he figured he wasn't going to get a choice anyway.

"Hang on for all you're worth. Noreen needs an anchor. I'm guessing some part of her knows you can be that. So be that." The force of his last three words completely belied his unexpected welcome.

The message was clear.

Man up, asshole.

Coming home with Noreen, he'd just walked into a world he couldn't begin to understand. But now that he was here, he'd better figure it out fast.

* * *

"Holy shit!"

"Don't let Mom hear you speak like that," Noreen wondered what had amazed Xavier this time. He'd been wide-eyed ever since they'd climbed off the helicopter. He'd hardly said a word through dinner. Not able to help with cleanup one-handed, though it had earned him points with Mama for trying, he had retreated out the back door into the night. She followed as fast as she could.

It was good—give her family a little time to talk about them. Their nerves at Xavier's sudden presence in their midst were almost as much of a jumble as her own.

What had she been thinking when she'd invited Sergeant Xavier Jones to Muskogee, Oklahoma? According to Connie, she'd been thinking the impossible. There was no way she'd found "the one" and there was even more no way that "the one" was Xavier Jones.

"I've never seen so many stars."

Noreen studied his outline against the Milky Way; he was looking up.

"Mama Bee already offered me a bar of soap with my strawberry cobbler and ice cream.

She said two Army mouths in the house were already four too many. Apparently Connie doesn't count because she almost never speaks. I think washing my mouth out with soap was a joke. I'm hoping."

"You know there is something you could do."

"What's that?" Xavier didn't look down.

"You could kiss me."

"I could," he agreed amiably without turning to her.

She considered punching his arm. The bad one.

"But if I start, how am I supposed to ever stop?"

Noreen wasn't sure of the answer to that one either.

Then an owl swooped by low enough to make Xavier duck at the hard flap of wings close by.

"What the hell?"

"Just a barn owl. She lives up over the harvester bay. Don't worry, you're too big to interest her any." She looked back to see if anyone was watching out the windows…which was ridiculous because they were far enough into the yard for it to be pitch dark. She could see her family moving about in the kitchen. Faint laughter on the breeze that she'd take as a good sign.

She turned back to the night and slipped an arm around Xavier's waist. His good arm wrapped about her shoulders. They watched the stars together for a long time before he spoke again.

"I've never seen *family* before. Seriously, these aren't a bunch of actors you hired for my benefit?"

"Nope. With all the good, the bad, and the weird, they're real."

"So you've got a white sister-in-law who's closer than your real one. One big brother ready to push me out of the helo, another that thinks whatever we do it's going to be damned fun to watch, and a father who seriously knows how to lay down a threat."

"Paps threatened you? He's never done that to anyone."

Xavier squeezed her shoulder more tightly. "These people love you so much they can't help themselves. You're the youngest, their precious little girl."

"I was an accident."

"A what?"

"Late birth. Unexpected."

"Seems to make you all the more special in their eyes."

Noreen decided that Xavier was a pretty astute observer.

"I'm guessing they can tell I'm thinking pretty much the same thing about you. Probably the only reason they didn't haul out the rifles, yet."

"What are you doing to me, Xavier?" Noreen rested her head against his shoulder.

He was silent for a long time. She was content to just stand by him and watch the night.

The house lights blinked off one by one. Mama

hadn't even suggested moving the kids around to make a guest room. She and Xavier had never slept together and now her family just assumed they would be.

In Balad it would have been much…simpler. Meet at the shuttered USO. Get some glorious sexual relief and have a shared secret that would cheer them both up until the next time. With Xavier she had no doubt about the sex being good enough that there'd be a next time.

Now it was all confused. She'd never had a boy in her bedroom. She'd been caught in more than one neighbor's hayloft, but never in her own home. They were going to sleep together, but now it meant so much more that…

"Maybe we could just stand out here all night."

Xavier soft chuckle made her relax a little. "Sudden case of nerves?"

"Not about you," and it was true. "But about you in my family home with my family knowing… yeah. That's being a bit of a stretch."

"We're on a farm. In the movies that means a hayloft."

"No cattle or horses, so no hayloft." Had he been reading her mind?

"There goes my James Bond fantasy moment."

"Well, you're just going to have to replace it with something else, I guess." No real surprise that Xavier would be thinking about Mr. Smooth tumbling the sexy, busty Honor Blackman in a pile of hay in *Goldfinger.*

"How about this for an even better fantasy?" And he pulled her through a half turn until her chest was pressed up against his arm in the sling and bent down to kiss her.

It wasn't with the fiery need like at the USO, or the stolen moment while stocking the helo. Oh, the need was there. She could feel it vibrating through her fingertips where they'd landed on his chest. An electrical conduction between their nervous systems that hit like a full milligram jolt of adrenaline—enough to restart her heart even though it was already racing.

But Xavier was right about one thing, his kiss was straight out of a fantasy. More caress than kiss.

Nobody kissed her that way, nor did she them. Kisses were the prelude to sex—or at least to teasing about sex. Or about teasing period, when there wasn't a chance there was going to be sex.

Xavier wrapped one arm around her and held her close. Her instincts and her past experience were in a rush, but her body was content to do little more than relax like a sigh as his lips trailed down her neck.

* * *

Xavier wasn't sure who he was trying to reassure. Noreen, that he really did understand where her nerves were coming from—this being her family home and all. Or himself, that he couldn't want a woman this much and it wasn't somehow wrong.

He tried to lift his other arm around her because he wanted, he needed to hold her close. Somehow this fantasy moment *might* slip away and he wanted to hold on as hard as possible.

But the strap on his sling caught Noreen under the chin and elicited a "Gurk!" of harsh reality.

"Sorry."

"Talk about breaking the mood, Xavier."

He started to remove the sling and she slapped at his hand.

"Do not do that. Doctor's orders."

"Shit, woman. Are you telling me we aren't going to do this until my shoulder heals? Don't like the sound of that none."

"No. I'm telling you that you keep your god-damned arm in the sling."

Reaching for her in the dark, this time he caught a handful of breast. Not what he was aiming for, but on Noreen, that was a very good thing and he wasn't about to let go. Palm to her breast, he curled his fingers under her arm and this time she ended up with her back pressed against his front.

Maybe this wasn't such a good idea. He could feel himself nestling right into the curve of her lower back and the heat shot through him.

"Umm…" she eased away.

"Shit!" It was all getting awkward as hell and he didn't know what to do about it.

Noreen took his hand from her breast, but she didn't let go. Instead, she led him through the darkness, up the porch steps, and into the now silent house.

The stairs creaked loudly as they snuck up them, still holding hands. At the far end of a short hall, she opened a door and warned him to duck.

It was a good thing she did. When she turned on the light, it revealed a low bedroom tucked under the eaves. She could stand up in most of it without a problem, but his head kept brushing against the ceiling. Half-height closets were built into the lowest part of the room and the rest was dominated by a big bed. Not a king size, but plenty big for them to do what he wanted to do—if he wasn't injured.

The paint was a warm yellow, the rug worn, and a big quilt covered the bed in crazy patches of color. Into each patch—with edges that were anything but straight—were sewn diagrams that must be farm life. Ears of corn, a tractor, a bundle of wheat, and a hundred other images that all looked…farmy. The pieces were held together by crazy stitching, the same color yellow as the walls, but that looked different in every seam.

This was…a cozy bedroom. Cozy.

His bedroom at Fort Benning had been a barracks. In Prichard, he slept in a car as often as not on someone's ratted out sofa. And his childhood bedroom had been snipped right out of *Architectural Digest*—no mess allowed.

Ever.

A sock on his own floor could get him

grounded. His very first memory was being told not to mess up his room.

"I—" even whispering, his voice sounded strange here and it forced him to silence.

Then he remembered that Larry had said his little sister never brought home a boyfriend.

He forgot how to breathe.

She started to undo his sling. Her hands, dancing so close to his arm—he shifted back a step and bumped up against a low dresser. That had him startling forward like some damned pinball and he knocked his head against the ceiling lamp. He turned for the door and snagged a foot in the heavy throw rug, a giant oval spiral in grays, reds, and browns.

Everything spoke of her cozy refuge. Her belonging.

But not him.

Noreen's hand on his arm stopped him from floundering into the wall and waking the whole house.

Women were easy. If they were willing, a good feel, some hot kissing, and a hard bang at the end.

Women were easy… Noreen was not. Here everything meant something.

First boyfriend she's ever brought home.

The little white chick—uh, Connie—warning him with those serious eyes.

Noreen needs an anchor. So be that.

He turned back to face her surroundings. This room filled with family history and a childhood.

An aged, and much loved red-and-white bunny rabbit perched in the place of honor on the tiny nightstand. Pictures of birds on the walls.

The homey quilt.

Xavier managed to open his mouth, but couldn't think of what do with it once he had.

He finally turned back toward Noreen. He'd apologize, make some excuse, and go sleep in the barn even if there wasn't any hay.

But she—

"Holy crap!"

* * *

"Keep your voice down," she whispered as she tossed aside her t-shirt and bra.

Xavier just stared. It sent a flush of heat to her cheeks, but Noreen ignored that. His eyes wide, he stared like he wanted to devour her.

"I can't take your weight if I'm on my back— I'm still too sore. And you can't hold yourself up with your bad arm. So I hope you don't mind if I'm on top." Even after she'd shed her sneakers and socks, he only stared.

Occasionally his eyes traveled down her body, but for the most part he was just watching her all at once, from head to toes.

"Are you planning to get undressed?"

"I…dunno," Xavier kept his voice down this time, but it was so deep that it still seemed to vibrate through her and echo about the room.

"What do you mean?"

"I mean this room is being exposed to some serious damn perfection at the moment. Me getting naked is gonna be a major downgrade."

"I'll be the judge of that," she eased off his sling, then pushed him to sit on the bed so that she could pull off his t-shirt without hurting him. Most guys just stared at her breasts and said how great they were. But though Xavier certainly looked at them, he spent more time looking at her face.

It was strange undressing him. He was as passive as an unconscious patient, letting her do what was needed. But she wasn't exposing a wound for treatment. Without his t-shirt, Xavier's powerful chest and arms were on full display. He looked like he could move mountains. And he was vibrantly conscious, his big muscles rippling beneath that luscious skin with every motion.

"Uh," the impact of his half-naked presence was so strong she wasn't so sure of herself.

She'd yanked off her own t-shirt and bra in an attempt to make this just about sex. But Xavier hadn't gone there.

So she'd try again. Stripping off his pants would definitely change the focus to the physical. But before she could even undo his belt, he snagged her around the waist with his good arm and hauled them together. Forcing her to straddle his lap. Hard enough to knock half the air out of her lungs.

The other half went away at the sensation of her bare chest against his.

Even using only one arm, he held her so tightly that she could barely breathe.

"You sure about this, Noreen?" he whispered in her ear. "Really sure? This is your home, your family, your bedroom. I've slept on plenty of couches before."

"Since when did you turn out to be such a decent guy?"

"Alien abduction? Maybe they reprogrammed my brain while neither of us was watching. Those docs in Balad? Maybe they did some shit to me, 'cause it sure doesn't sound like me to be holding the most beautiful woman to ever come my way and then offer her a way out."

"It doesn't sound like me to bring a man into my family's home. But if you keep running your hand up and down my back like that, you're going to convince me it was a good idea."

He did it again, from the base of her spine, all the way up in one long stroke, over her shoulders, up into her hair, and back down. His hand was so big that it seemed to cover the whole width of her back.

She wrapped her arms around his neck, lay her head on his shoulder, and gave in to the sensation as he eased still-sore muscles with his gentle caress. When he scooped his hand over her jeans, he was gentle enough that her injured behind didn't even twinge.

The entire rest of their first time making love felt just like that.

Xavier didn't treat her as if she was fragile, but he never forgot about her humiliating tailbone injury, instead using his hands around her waist to pull them together.

She'd been right that sex with Xavier would be well worth repeating. What she hadn't been right about was how incredible it would actually be.

Rough, fun, filled with friendly wrestling and powerful urges. Like Parkour in a bed: athletic, unpredictable, halfway to flying.

It was none of those.

Instead it was gentle, without being soft. It was potent, without being forceful.

And when she finally sheathed him and they came together, it was completely overwhelming.

Taking all of Xavier's length into her body wasn't merely about the physical sensation of an arousal greater than any she'd ever felt. It was about a body-spanning sensation of being filled: as if the rest of her became complete in that moment.

Noreen could only look down at him in wonder as her nervous system flashed overload warnings all up and down her body.

Splendid, pounding, glorious sensations fired through every corner of her autonomic and somatic nervous systems until they peaked in a series of jumbled noise.

A flash brighter than the explosion that had blown her through the air.

So bright, she had to close her eyes or be made blind.

She floated as nerve endings fired in random clusters, unable to communicate so much pleasure coherently.

Some infinite time later, she returned to her body enough to realize they were far from done.

Another section of her nervous system—she couldn't remember which part—that base level of instinctive animal, rocked her hips to coax more from the man so deep within her. That in turn sent more happy endorphins shooting up her body.

Never, in all of the med classes necessary to be a CSAR medic, had she so clearly understood what her body was capable of doing.

Of feeling.

Of wanting.

Because, oh god, did she ever *want* in this moment.

Xavier's release did not free her from this awareness, it freed her from *all* awareness until she merely floated on the waves coursing through her body. Through their body—they were clearly one. Never had she felt so connected to anyone or anything, not even herself, as she was to the oneness that was them.

* * *

Xavier wasn't sure if aliens really had gotten to him.

Women were for sex. It was that simple. He'd proven it time and again. Sometimes it was really good sex and they'd stick around each other as long as it stayed that way…days, weeks, a couple of times for months. There was one that lasted almost a year—he might have married her if she hadn't demanded he leave the Army as part of it. The sex with Feleysa had been good, but it wasn't that kind of good.

It was all just sex.

Until now.

Noreen Wallace, in her childhood bedroom, didn't have a single thing to do with sex—at least not how he'd ever understood it.

His body had released into her so hard that it would have been painful if it hadn't felt so good. She'd done something, he'd be damned if he knew what, that was way outside his experience—and he'd thought he'd had a world of experience. This Oklahoma farm girl had just showed him how he was an idiot.

There was some other level of shit going on though, even if he couldn't pin it down.

Being with Noreen wasn't merely more powerful than anything in his past. It was more… important. Lame-ass word, but the best he had.

When he finally could focus, he looked up at her. Arched over him like she was the maiden on the bow of some old ship, her breasts stood out prominently, bold and ready to go. Her long neck, which he was starting to think just might be the best feature of her spectacular body, rose in a slender arch. And her face was frozen in a conflict of emotions that looked much like the pain-and-pleasure that had wracked through him moments ago.

She wasn't breathing, just holding the pose in a fiercely tight clench that went all the way down to where he was buried in her.

A short, hard gasp shook her body. Then another. Each sent a shockwave down to where she kept her hips pressed tightly against his.

Then between one moment and the next, she collapsed down onto his chest and groaned softly.

"What did you just do to me, Xavier?"

He kissed the top of her head, "Dunno. But I sure hope that we can figure out how to do that again."

"Maybe," her voice was shaky as she raised her head enough to plant a kiss in the middle of his chest before dropping her head back down. "But maybe I'll never recover from that. If so, then we'll just have to remember how you overloaded my nervous system one day and I could never fix it."

Xavier had learned it was a good idea—especially if he wanted future sex—to confirm that it had been good sex for her as well. He liked that Noreen didn't make him ask the question which sometimes got awkward or false answers that he could never figure out what to do with.

Except this had nothing to do with sex.

It was like all that physical pleasure was just the sidewalk. He was on some main road, in a carjacked Porsche, headed full speed to… He had no idea where.

What had *he* done to *her*?

Shit, woman!

What had *she* done to *him*?

He seriously didn't know, but whatever it was, one thing was clear.

No way in hell was Xavier Jones ever letting go of this woman.

He wrapped his good arm around her, hugged her just hard enough to elicit a happy squeak, then let the very long day, the great sex, and all of the emotions he didn't understand pound him into sleep.

Chapter 8

Wake-up sex had never been a priority for Noreen, that was more of a guy thing. But slowly climbing to consciousness all wrapped up in a big, powerful lover, it shot straight to the top of her list.

Teasing him awake had been fun. His arousal was most of the way to full before he'd become conscious enough to be aware of it.

"Shit! Thought I was dreaming."

She'd then done her best to show him that he was.

Now Noreen sat on her doughnut-shaped pillow and smiled down into her oatmeal at the breakfast table. Dreamy ran through her body like it was never going away. Being back in the family kitchen only added to it. The old fake brick linoleum floor had been replaced with new fake brick linoleum. The cupboards were worn with age and clean with care. It was dominated by the big table that saw every meal, a thousand childhood projects, and far more laughter than tears.

"Morning," Connie sat down next to her with her own oatmeal.

"You make it the same way Grumps did," and Noreen felt the pain of her grandfather's death all over again. Grumps' last night had been the day Noreen graduated ROTC and was made an officer in the Army. Five years that had passed too quickly.

Connie nodded. "I only knew him for those last few days, but I always do it this way so that I remember him." Finely diced apple cooked in, a drizzle of maple syrup on top, and three dried apricots slivered and sprinkled in for "zing".

"Did you tell them your news last night?" Noreen needed a subject change.

"Did she tell us what?" Mama Bee strolled into the kitchen and poured some coffee.

Connie just shook her head.

"Nothing, sorry," Noreen went for her best innocent look.

Mama gave them both the look that said that wasn't going to work. She shooed a cat out of her chair and sat down at the battered old table.

Noreen traced a finger over the old scorch mark from when she'd served her first-ever scrambled eggs to everyone by setting the hot pan of scorched eggs directly on the table. "Remember when—"

"Not going to work with me, Noreen Wallace. Now what are you two gals up to that I'm not allowed to know about yet? This about you and that handsome young man? Was he as good to you as I'm hoping?"

"Mama!"

She just did her innocent shrug thing, which told Noreen exactly where she'd gotten that skill—only Mama did it more convincingly.

Connie didn't look up to give her any help.

Noreen sighed, "No. He was better than that."

"Good," Mama nodded as if she'd known it would and that somehow made everything right with the world.

And it did, with one part of the world. But it messed up a whole other part of it. Noreen wasn't supposed to feel this way about any man.

"Looking mighty flustered for someone who I'm sure had herself a nice portion of some wake-up sex for breakfast. And," Mama aimed her gaze at Connie, "don't think that Nori's sexual triumphs are distracting me from you not telling me something. If ever I had a white girl come out of these hips, you know I'd wish it was you. So tell me."

Noreen was close enough to see that Connie was blushing even though she'd shaken her shoulder-length hair forward to cover her face as she kept studying her oatmeal.

"She can't, Mama." Then Noreen nudged her sister-in-law in the ribs. "Not until after she's told John."

Connie's head bolted up and Mama broke out in a peal of laughter. They were all smiling at each other when John stumbled in. He beelined for the coffee pot, apparently unaware of the three women watching him as he poured, added cream and sugar, and took his first sip before offering a deep contented sigh.

"Johnny," Mama Bee called out to him.

"Uh-huh. Morning, Mama. Hey, Trouble." He mussed Noreen's hair and for once she let him get away with it. Then he wandered over and kissed Connie on top of the head. "Need a refresher on your coffee?"

"Nope," was all Connie said.

"She really shouldn't," Noreen couldn't resist, earning her Connie's scowl. During the helicopter flight yesterday, they had talked about reducing caffeine—one cup and one soda per day, max.

"Definitely not," Mama was watching John.

"You okay, babe?" John squatted down until he was eye level with Connie.

She nodded, but she started crying.

"What's with the tears? You never cry. She never cries," he looked around the table as if seeking confirmation. "Only time I've ever seen her cry was over Grumps' passing."

"You going to tell him, Connie, or do I?"

"Hush, Nori," Mama's voice was sharp.

Connie tried to speak, but nothing came out. She finally just threw her arms around John's shoulders and hung on. Her sister-in-law didn't speak much, but she'd never had a problem before when there was something to say.

John's eyes were round and worried when he looked at Noreen over Connie's shoulder.

"What happening?" he mouthed to her.

Taking pity on him, Noreen cradled her arms and made a rocking motion.

John pushed Connie back enough that he could see her face. "Really?"

Connie nodded quickly and the tears kept flowing.

John scooped his wife up, sat in the chair himself, and cradled her in his lap. He buried his face in her hair and the two of them just sat there holding on to each other as Mama dabbed at her own tears.

* * *

Xavier wasn't exactly sure what he'd just walked in on.

Good or bad?

Ask if he could help or just hit the door at a sprint and don't stop running until he hit the next county? He couldn't tell.

Connie was curled up in Big John's lap and he was holding her like she was dead or something. Noreen's mother was wiping at her eyes with a dishtowel. And Noreen's eyes—not exactly dry either—looked up at him with a seriously puzzled expression. Sort of a *Who the hell are you?* kinda vibe.

He went to back away as Larry shoved him from behind.

"What in the world?" Paps came in behind Larry and the three of them were now lined up looking at the crying scene going on in the kitchen.

"Got me," Xavier whispered it softly.

Noreen was still looking at him like he really had just beamed down from another planet.

"What?" he mouthed at her.

She just shook her head.

No longer than a shower ago they'd been going at each other like they'd invented sex themselves. And now it's like he was…a total stranger.

Well he didn't need that kind of shit. He knew women who got all weird about the morning after. *Great sex, honey. But my family needs to still think I'm a virgin.* Or some such crap.

Larry and Paps moved further into the room.

Xavier wasn't dumb enough to follow. He turned and went through the front room and out the front door. He ignored the burst of noise and shouts from behind him.

It was harder to ignore the sound of running feet, especially because he was out in the middle of fucking nowhere. The field past the equipment barn stretched on forever with waist-high wheat.

Out of options, he planted his feet on the tire-chewed earth that separated yard from field.

"Where are you going?"

"Nowhere," and wasn't that an ugly truth.

"What do you have against babies?"

"I've got a problem with women who— Wait! What? How did babies get in the middle of this?" He turned to look down at Noreen. She was standing fist on hips in shorts, a light t-shirt, and sneakers. Knowing now exactly what hid under even those scanty clothes made him hungry for more. Looking at her expression said it wasn't gonna be happening anytime soon. *Shit!*

"You heard me," her voice still grated with fury. It definitely had a military snap to it.

"Babies?"

"Yes. Connie is going to have one. You've heard of them, haven't you? Little beings who grow up into bigger ones?"

"Connie? Seriously? John's kid?"

"If it's someone else's, I'll kick her ass. You ask that question around anyone else in the family, I'll kick yours. And don't smirk, I can take your ass down anytime I want. In or out of a sling."

"Babies," he repeated to buy himself a little time. Noreen wasn't the sort of person to underestimate. "She happy about it?"

"What do you think? They're all in there celebrating and I'm out here with you because—I don't know why. What the hell is your problem, Jones?" It was his first view of Noreen the angry woman. She was always so positive, such a cheery determined force in any group and on any flight, that the contrast was shocking. Not the nasty bitch kind of angry, but more F5-tornado-ready-to-kick-your-ass-but-good.

"What the hell do you want from me?"

All she did was glare at him.

"You wanta know what I think about babies? Fine! Where I came from, babies are *bad* news. The whores had to scrape up the cash for an abortion if they wanted to keep working, but after four or five times it gets risky as hell. Women wanting a sugar daddy would get pregnant any way they could. I always used my own condoms so that the women couldn't pinprick 'em and set me up. Babies are a goddamn trap."

Noreen just gaped at him. Then she spun on her heel and walked away.

Xavier had never felt so helpless in his life. He wanted her like he'd never wanted a woman. She was confusing the crap out of him.

But she didn't go back to the house or over to the barn. She just walked away, giving him a fine view of her exceptional ass and long legs. *Don't be thinking 'bout that, dude.* It was tricky. Women were always one thing, but—

Noreen turned and walked back toward him offering him another fine view, though she continued to scowl at the ground as she moved. When she reached him, she didn't look up…might have run right into him if he hadn't stepped aside. She headed off along the churned track where the dirt was chewed up by turning tractor tires.

Like that time atop the wall at Balad, he followed because he didn't know what else to do. The land was flatter than a Balad Air Base runway. Soon they were walking between sorghum so tall he couldn't see a thing to one side and still-green wheat so expansive that there was no horizon in the other, just mesmerizing ripples as the wind waved through the field.

Around the end of the sorghum field he stumbled to a halt.

A patch of magnolia trees in bloom was such a shocking contrast in color that it felt like a pink-and-red slap. The ground was covered in the blooms. The air was so thick with the trees' perfume that he almost felt drunk. He wandered into the middle of the grove and slowly turned around and around. A gentle morning breeze slipped one petal and then another off their branches to flutter down to the pink carpet that covered the ground.

"It's like magic."

There was no reply.

He turned and looked once more. He was alone. No sign of Noreen. Somehow, between one moment and the next she'd disappeared. As if she'd evaporated into thin air.

Looking up, he spotted her watching him from high in the limbs of the next tree over. No way he'd be climbing up after her, even if both of his arms were working.

He sat, placing his back against the nearest

tree, and just let the beauty of the occasional falling petal fill the time. One thing Xavier had learned flying CSAR was patience. Even while others fought, it was his job to simply wait and be ready. If Noreen thought she could outwait him, she had another think coming.

One moment she was in the tree, the next she was standing not a pace beyond his stretched-out feet—one of her acrobatic moves. Even with a broken tush, her every move called to him. But she didn't speak. And that was a waiting game he expected he was going to lose, so he didn't bother trying.

"You're gonna tell me all the wonders of babies. You're going to be an aunt. Well just remember, Connie and John gave up flying for the Night Stalkers to have a kid. And what happens to her career when she's got one, or two? I don't see how a kid is a good thing."

And then Noreen had that breakfast-table look again. Like *he* was the alien here.

"Do you want babies, Noreen? Not gonna be doing your CSAR Parkour shit with an eight-month bulge. You ever think about that?"

"But it doesn't mean I don't want them," her voice was as soft as the falling blooms.

"Welcome to them."

"But not you," she didn't make it a question. And that look solidified into something hard and he knew what it meant this time: he *was* the outsider here.

He was sick of not belonging.

Working at the chop shop in Prichard had fit—at least until the recruiter fished him out.

He'd belonged in the Army and then the Night Stalkers.

Xavier knew who he was in those places.

But his parents' home?

This place?

"I shouldn't even be here," he thumped his head back against the tree, feeling the rough bark on his shaved scalp. He closed his eyes to block out Noreen's baleful stare.

By the time he opened them, he was alone.

Chapter 9

"She's gone to a friend's."

Yeah, Xavier knew what that shit meant. Until he was out of the way, Noreen wasn't going to come home to her family. He packed his duffel and slung it over his good shoulder. He tried to think of some note to leave on her pillow.

Good luck with the kids?

You were the best fuck of my life?

*I'm gonna think of you every—*he really had to get out of here.

Back downstairs, he found John by himself in the kitchen.

"Can I get a lift out of here?"

"Sure, where you going?" John blinked at him in surprise. Then scowled when he spotted Xavier's duffel.

"How the hell would I know? Bus station? Airport? Somewhere not here."

"You don't want to be doing that," John rose to his feet looking massive and some kind of pissed.

"You're right. I don't. But your little sister has different ideas on that. I just got my walking papers."

"She—"

"Look," Xavier was trying to do the right thing. "She wants me gone. Record long relationship, lasted a night and part of a morning too. Best that ever happened to a shit like me. Now it's done. You gonna help me clear out or do I start walkin' before she comes after me with a squirrel gun?"

"I've seen the way she looks at you."

"No, you haven't."

"Connie walked out of here because she thought she shouldn't be here. It almost killed me."

"Well, this time's different. I'd be staying if it was up to me. Your sister gave me my DD Form 214 Report of Separation. Court martial. Dishonorable. The whole nine yards. Loathing doesn't begin to cover it."

John finally sighed, grabbed a set of keys by the kitchen door, and held the door for Xavier.

The entire drive to the Muskogee bus station passed in silence.

When Xavier started to climb down, John stopped him with a hand on his arm.

"You sure about this?"

Xavier didn't even try to speak past the knot in his gut. He managed a nod.

"Bus will see you up to Tulsa International. Can go where you please from there," John held out a hand.

After a long moment's consideration, Xavier shook it, then turned for the ticket window.

Somewhere behind him John's voice said, "Sorry, man."

Yeah, that pretty much covered it.

* * *

Noreen didn't know what she was feeling when she got back to the house that night. Numb? Lost? Wrung out? That last one she was used to after the brutal workouts and trials necessary to make it into Special Operations. But this was different. All she'd done was sit with her sister Janice and talk. Even playing with her young niece and nephew hadn't cheered her up the way it usually did. Somehow it had made her feel worse.

The porch light was off and everyone was in bed by the time she crawled out of Mama's car.

"You're out late," Connie's voice sounded from the darkness over by the porch swing.

"Is there a curfew now? Why aren't you up with your husband celebrating being parents?" Noreen sat on Mama's rocker, only wincing a little at the pain, and could just barely make out Connie in the darkness. The moon was up and bright, but it came from the other side of the house, lighting the yard but casting the deep porch in impenetrable shadow. No owl to cheer up the evening. No crickets. Like the world had crawled into some dark hole.

"I'm here so that John isn't the one waiting for you."

"I wish he'd stop treating me like I was twelve."

"Never going to happen, Noreen. You know that. He loves you too much."

She figured that was a truth. John would always be overprotective and there was a part of her that would always appreciate it.

"Doesn't mean he wouldn't be chewing you out at the top of his lungs at the moment."

"Say what?"

"Why did you boot Xavier down the road? I think that's the real question."

"I didn't do that. He just doesn't understand about…" Her throat went dry. "Down the road? What do you mean *down the road?*" She couldn't stop the note of hysteria she could feel climbing out of her own throat.

Connie's sigh spoke volumes, then she muttered a soft curse. Connie never cursed. This was bad.

"What do you mean—" she couldn't finish it.

Years ago Connie had insisted on leaving against John's wishes. And Noreen had been the one to drive her to town. It had ripped out her heart, but saying "no" to Connie hadn't been an option.

"But you knew," Noreen railed at her. "From the time it was you leaving. How could you let him go?"

"John drove him to town—"

"I'm gonna kill him," Noreen jolted her feet.

"—because Xavier said you wouldn't come home until he was gone. He told John that he wanted to stay, but you'd told him to go."

"I never said that."

"John said he used the word 'loathing,' and that you issued him a DD Form 214."

"I—" she sank back into her mother's chair. "Did I?"

Connie waited in the darkness that swirled around Noreen until she felt seasick.

"No. He was the one who got all strange. You saw him. He just walked out when you said you were going to have a baby." Or had he been in the room for that? No, he'd stared at *her* not Connie, looking at her like she herself had…slapped him?

"I was focusing on other things," Connie was still back in some earlier part of the conversation.

"Well, he did," and that made more sense than anything else she could think of. "And when I confronted him on it, everything got all confused. He tossed in my face that having babies and working CSAR didn't go together. Then I asked if he wanted kids. You know what he said? He said he shouldn't even be here."

Again Connie did one of her silence things.

Noreen had learned to give Connie room to order her thoughts and kept her mouth shut. How could Xavier be gone? One minute she'd been sitting at the kitchen table, imagining what it would be like to hold his child, their child—Connie wasn't the only one having a life-changing moment this morning. The next he was chucking the fighting woman's dilemma of career versus family in her face as if it was *her* fault or as if she had all the answers.

"You can't imagine what you have here, Noreen."

"Here?"

"This farm. This family. Don't forget, I came into this family as an orphan; it sounds as if Xavier might as well be. You can't imagine how strange all this is to people like us. Even if you could imagine yourself without any family or relations, you still wouldn't get how it feels. Family—any family, never mind one like yours—is a shining light that you've never seen before, blinding you worse than rocket flare in night vision. There's no way you can belong to that light, ever. As an orphan, as an outsider, you know this for a fact. I knew it, right down to my bones."

"But you belong here."

Connie's nod was just visible. "You won't believe this, and I'm glad for you. I got that only this morning. I'm going to have a child who will be part of this family. That makes me understand in a way I never could before that I too belong here."

"But I love you. John loves you. Mama, Paps… Grumps loved you. How could you not know?"

"It's different, Noreen, trust me. I know I'm *welcome* here, which surprises and humbles me every day. I'm only now starting to understand that I *belong* here as well. That's after *five years.* Xavier didn't even have twenty-four hours. Do you remember your first flight into a battle?"

"Remember? Scared the crap out of me. I couldn't seem to make sense of what was happening. If I'd had to recover someone who was wounded I don't know if I could have even treated them—they'd probably have bled out from a gut shot I didn't notice while I was bandaging a cut finger. Everything was happening at…once…oh."

"Your family's home is where everything makes sense to you. Trust me that none of it made sense to Xavier."

"None of it?" Connie was right, she couldn't imagine what that was like.

"Except maybe you."

"And when I imagined having his children and couldn't make sense of that…"

"He suddenly lost his sole frame of reference here. You can really imagine that with him?"

"I can, I could." Noreen rested a hand on her belly and imagined what that would feel like. It was surprisingly easy. "I can."

Connie reached out and clasped her hand hard.

"I need to talk to him," Noreen looked around the moonlit yard of her home as if she might spot him. But he wasn't here.

"So call him."

She had her phone halfway out before the truth sank in. "I don't know his number."

"Where would he go?"

"He only has one place." Beamed down into the Army on the first day. Captain Luc had no past.

Noreen closed her eyes to the cool moonlight that washed over the yard and the fields. The one good thing about her injury was that she would get to recuperate at home. Two weeks here was a pure gift. A gift to her. But to Xavier it would be—

"I have to get back to Balad."

Chapter 10

Xavier sat in the white rental Camry and waited. The dawn was soft, warming the sky, but not yet raising the muggy heat that he knew would follow.

It had taken him a while to find the place. Over a dozen years had passed since he'd been here last. Back then his transport was by bicycle, not by car, and the change was confusing.

The sycamores had grown and the big cottonwood was gone, but he finally found it. Kingsway, Country Club neighborhood, Mobile, Alabama. In the eight years since joining the Army, the closest he'd been to his parents' home was three hours away while flight training at Fort Rucker. And four years before that had been on the other side of Mobile—both physically and metaphorically—in Prichard.

"What the hell are you doing here, Xavier?"

"No fuckin' idea."

Answering himself in an empty car. Real bad sign that he was losing it.

Coming back to this neighborhood, an even worse one.

He remembered the fight when he'd announced he was leaving, at age fourteen. All three of them screaming at each other. His father, never a man of action despite his size, clenching his hands impotently. The sharp, slicing pain of his mother's slap as she declared he was no son of hers. He could still feel the outline of her blow on his cheek.

Xavier had left behind everything he knew, climbed into his father's BMW, and raced it away. They'd so wanted him to be what he wasn't—a white-boy genius willing to kowtow to fit in. In Country Club, their neighborhood, the one-percenters were blacks—two thousand whites in massive homes and twenty blacks. He was the only one his age in school and the other kids made it real damn clear how welcome he wasn't. Even the teachers didn't give a shit about him.

He'd never driven before and ran his dad's Beemer into a Mercedes coming out of a driveway not a mile later. Airbags blown in both cars, he'd managed to walk away. Hid while the police cruisers circled.

Nine miles away in Prichard, the whites were the one-percenters. He'd been down with that.

As the sun came up, he tried to remember

the angry kid storming out of the two-story brick colonial complete with Greek revival columns. It was hard, not because he didn't remember, but rather because he did.

Like his father, he hadn't been a fighter. And unlike the white boys in school, his skin was dark enough to hide the bruises. The school principal hadn't even listened, suspending his ass for—while he was being beaten—managing to deliver a pair of black eyes to the worst bullies in the school, twin sons of the wealthiest bastard in Mobile.

His mother's slap had landed hard on top of the mass of pain that was his jaw.

He could feel her jawbone break beneath his fist when he'd hit her back.

Could still remember her cry as she fell to the oak parquet of the kitchen floor.

The house was twice the size of the Wallace's farmhouse, maybe more. And it was as cold as the marble entryway.

The front door opened. Mom and Dad came out, looking older than he imagined possible. Dad was going gray, and Mom's dress was matronly rather than the flashy designer-wear she'd always insisted on. Her hairstyle was severe and did not compliment her bone-thin sharp features.

And then a little black girl, no more than ten, came out the door and closed it carefully behind her. She wore a pink pinafore that looked right out of some old history book. She didn't move like a kid—she moved like a ghost. *I'm invisible. I'm invisible.* He could practically hear her mantra.

He wasn't sure what he'd planned to do. Confront them? At least force them to look at him once?

But how could he do that in front of his little sister?

He had a little sister!

Did she even know he existed? Or was she as oblivious as he'd been?

Dad climbed in his late-model Beemer and Mom loaded her daughter into a Cadillac SUV so new he could smell if from across the road despite having his windows up.

Xavier could only watch them all go.

Mom went the other way, but Dad drove in his direction.

His eyes tracked to Xavier as he came even with where Xavier was parked in the rental-white Camry.

Then he flinched with recognition, but kept going.

Xavier didn't know why he was surprised when the cops showed up less than two minutes later.

Chapter 11

Noreen sat atop the T-wall above the closed USO club on Balad Air Base. Atop the wall and her stupid doughnut pillow. Her ass still hurt and the long flight back from Oklahoma hadn't helped it any.

Where the *hell* had Sergeant Xavier Jones gotten to? He hadn't reported back in. She'd ponied up the money to call Washington State, but the 5th Battalion liaison had said that Xavier hadn't come through security on the battalion's Fort Lewis base.

She couldn't call every recruiter in Mobile asking if they knew Xavier. Besides, the two guys he knew had probably rotated back to their units. Or retired. Or, with the way her luck was running, beamed back up to the mothership along with Xavier.

For the entire flight back and the long day she'd spent cooling her heels, she'd tried to figure out what to say to him. She knew it had to be… No. She didn't know what it had to be.

The commander wouldn't even put her back to work.

"This is a medical leave. Unless a doc signs off, I can't use you."

The doc had poked and prodded her, enough to elicit a yelp of pain despite her commitment to not reacting. The verdict of "not yet" had cut out any chance of finding distraction here. Not even light duty.

With the crew running at full tilt, they weren't helping her much either. They were somewhere out there in the darkness on a mission and she was roosting here with a sore butt.

Balad had become one of the dullest places on Earth.

She was even too sore to practice Parkour… Noreen had needed an old Hummer that had been parked close to the barrier wall to even climb atop the T-wall in the first place.

One of these days she'd…

"Heard that I'd find you here."

And there he was. Xavier was leaning against the wall looking up at her. His arm was still in a sling.

"Heard from who?"

"Connie."

"Connie? How did you hear from Connie?

Did she have your number and not tell me? I'm gonna—"

Xavier shook his head. "She told me when I showed back up at the house."

"You went back to— But I'm here in—" Noreen's head was going to implode. Her brain had clearly shriveled to the size of a walnut and her skull would collapse into the resulting vacuum at any moment.

Xavier was just nodding.

"Why did you go back? Where did you go?"

"How about we talk on the level?"

Even though she'd hunted him halfway around the globe, she wasn't sure that she wanted to do that. But she didn't see any other option.

She waved him to go around the front, then she carefully lowered herself down to the USO's rear deck and found her way through the darkness to open the locked front door for him.

He followed her back out to the deck in silence.

"Where did you go?" It wasn't the first question on her mind, but it felt far safer than asking why he'd gone.

* * *

Having told Noreen his real past, something not even his Army recruiter pals fully knew, he found it possible to tell her the rest of it.

It was maybe the hardest thing he'd ever done, telling Noreen all of the dirty truth. He couldn't read her face as he described that final night in his home. Punching out his own mother. It made him sound like a sadistic bastard. He couldn't even claim to not have hit someone since. Fighting wasn't a way of life in Prichard, but it was certainly a major pastime and he'd learned to give out better than he got, so that others left him alone.

"Didn't take me long to shed that in the Army though. Not many guys bigger than me, but plenty who were nastier. My last real fight was in the third week of Basic Training. I took offense at who knows what. Other guy was a street kid from Detroit—even if he looked like a blond Iowa farm boy—and was just as nasty as I was. For punishment, the drill sergeant had us paired on two-man drills for the rest of Basic. Learned he was a good guy. A really good one. Chad went Delta Force about a year before I went Night Stalkers."

Then he told her about discovering he had a little sister.

"Makes me want to go stage a rescue," Noreen whispered softly.

"Thought about it some, even as the cops were harassing me. Though one of them knew about the Night Stalkers and he backed off his partner pretty quick once he saw that's where I served."

"But…" she coaxed him back to the story.

"But," Xavier agreed. "How do I know she was trying to walk like she was invisible? Maybe she was trying to walk like a ninja or something. Maybe she likes pink and wanted to match her best friend in school. Maybe it was school picture day and she's normally dressed in punk-goth. That's when I got to thinking about you and me."

For the first time, Noreen really looked at him. Up to that point she'd been mostly looking down at the picnic table on the USO's old deck, brushing the sand gathered on the surface into shapes with little strokes of her fingertips.

"I saw what you were thinking of me. Hurt like goddamn hell, I'll have you know."

"I never—" She stopped when he held up a hand.

"That's what I figured out. You were looking at me in a damn weird way, but I never asked why because I *already knew*. Or thought I did. I can't ask my sister—at least not yet. Maybe when she's older. But I can ask you. So what the hell were you thinking that morning that made you look at me the way you did?"

Noreen went back to studying the sand, hard. Like it was the only thing in the world.

"Noreen. I just laid all my shit on the table. You can walk away from me if you want, but you better answer me first or I'm gonna get some kind of pissed."

* * *

"I was thinking of what it would be like to have your baby!" Noreen slapped a hand over her mouth. "I can't believe I just said that," she mumbled without removing her hand.

Apparently neither could Xavier as he just sat there with his jaw down.

When it got too ridiculous, she reached over with the hand that wasn't still covering her mouth and raised his jaw.

"I thought… Shit!" Xavier ran his good hand over his bare scalp.

"What?"

"I thought you were doing some kind of morning-after *I-so-don't-know-your-ugly-ass* kinda thing."

"After the amazing, life-altering sex we had, you think I'd feel that?"

Xavier had to admit that it hadn't made much sense at the time. It made even less now. He shrugged in self-defense, "It was one hell of a strange look."

"It was one hell of a strange feeling."

"So what did you decide?"

"Are you asking if I want to have your baby?"

Xavier blanched, which was good. At least she wasn't the only one here totally out of her depth. He shrugged uncertainly.

"Do you want to have kids at all?" she asked quickly because no way was she answering that question first.

"Never thought about it before, other than being careful during sex."

"Well think about it."

Xavier twisted his head to the side as if he had a sudden crick in his neck. "If you asked me forty-eight hours ago, it would have been an easy no."

She couldn't even manage the "But?" prompt.

"But then I saw my little sister, the one I didn't know I had, and I knew I'd missed some serious shit. It would have been cool to have a kid sister. She'd probably have been a total pain in the ass, just like John said you were."

"You talked to John about me?"

"Yeah, the whole family—when I went back to find you after driving ten hours each way to Mobile and back. Maybe the strangest meal I ever ate in my life—all that family gathered 'round like they really cared for each other."

"Nothing *like* about it. They really do," and again Noreen was proving his point. They really did, no matter how strange it was to witness.

"Anyway, he told a lot of Noreen stories. Then Mama Bee got in on it. They also told me about you going ROTC and turning officer in front of the whole family. You never saw people so damn proud. Only people at my Basic Training graduation were those two recruiters. Back then I thought they were just pleased with themselves for dragging another kid off the streets. Didn't know they'd keep being friends."

He fussed with his sling for a bit. Finally got up to walk around, but it didn't feel like he was trying to walk away, so Noreen sat and waited... and wished to hell she'd been at that meal. Partly to see and feel it, but also partly to stop the stories because she knew just which ones had been told.

"I talked to Connie and John afterward some, before I drove to the airport and headed here. Never seen two people so happy, swear to god I haven't. Made me wonder if my parents ever felt that way about me. Hard to imagine."

Then he came around the table and straddled the other end of the bench she was on. She could feel it flexing under her despite the doughnut pillow.

"At first I thought I'd never want a kid because I'd never want to have the disaster that was my family. Looking at John and Connie and your family? It'll take me a while to get used to the idea, but I can see it happening. I can see the kind of dad John will be. I'd never be that good, but I can see myself trying someday. Trying hard."

Like before, like that crazy morning, Noreen didn't know what was going on inside her. But she finally had some idea.

Xavier—big, powerful, beautiful Xavier—sat and waited patiently for her to figure out what she wanted. Even asking the question gave her the answer.

She scooted her doughnut pillow forward until they were knee-to-knee.

"I've always known I wanted kids someday. Right now I have too many things to do, but I've always known it. And now I know one other thing I really want."

"What's that?" Xavier took her two hands in his one big one when she reached out.

"I want them to be yours."

"Mine, huh?" Xavier rubbed his thumb over the back of her hands while he looked at her like no man ever had. His smile was brilliant in the dim light of the Balad USO's back deck—a place she'd never, ever forget.

All she could manage was a nod.

"Well, Miss Guardian, the thought of your kids being anyone else's makes me feel major crazy, so I guess they're going to *have* to be mine."

"You guess?"

"Your family makes me think that doing things in a traditional way has its points. So you're going to have to marry me first before we do any kid-making."

"Are you asking?" Noreen barely felt it as Xavier lifted her onto his lap with his good arm.

"Do I have to?"

"Yes."

"Is that a requirement or an answer to the question?"

"Yes," was all she could manage.

"Seems to me that knowing the answer takes some of the point out of my asking, but I'll do it for you. I'd do anything for you. Will you marry me and spend the rest of your days as the Guardian of my heart?"

Figuring that answering the same question again was redundant, she whispered softly against his lips, "Only if you'll be the Captain of mine."

His kiss was all the answer she ever needed.

About the Author

M.L. Buchman started the first of over 50 novels and now an equal number of short stories while flying from South Korea to ride his bicycle across the Australian Outback. Part of a solo around the world trip that ultimately launched his writing career.

All three of his military romantic suspense series—The Night Stalkers, Firehawks, and Delta Force—have had a title named "Top 10 Romance of the Year" by the American Library Association's Booklist. NPR and Barnes & Noble have named other titles "Top 5 Romance of the Year." In 2016 he was a finalist for Romance Writers of America prestigious RITA award. He also writes: contemporary romance, thrillers, and fantasy.

Past lives include: years as a project manager,

rebuilding and single-handing a fifty-foot sailboat, both flying and jumping out of airplanes, and he has designed and built two houses. He is now making his living as a full-time writer on the Oregon Coast with his beloved wife and is constantly amazed at what you can do with a degree in Geophysics. You may keep up with his writing and receive a free starter e-library by subscribing to his newsletter at: www.mlbuchman.com.

NSDQ (excerpt)
-a Night Stalkers CSAR story-

US Army Captain Lois Lang circled her Black Hawk helicopter five miles outside the battle zone and ten thousand feet up.

Usually height equaled safety in countries like Afghanistan where the Taliban had no air power, especially in the middle of the night. Get above the reach of most of the cheaper weapons—rifles, rocket-propelled grenades, and the like—and you were generally safe.

But the Lataband Pass, visible as a thousand shades of green in her night-vision gear, deep in the heart of the Hindu Kush Mountains, was at eight thousand feet and the surrounding peaks cleared ten easily. Even at night in the mountains, ten thousand was pushing the high-hot limit of the helicopters. The high altitude and mid-summer temperatures gave her helicopter's rotor blades thinner air to push against. To get higher, she'd have to really burn fuel; never a good bet on a long mission.

So, she and her crew circled wide and low, and watched their threat displays closely. Not a soul this far from the pass, not even a goatherd. Nothing to do but wait. Their job was CSAR—she always thought of a seesaw whenever she heard the acronym for Combat Search and Rescue, every time—which meant their night would be quiet and routine, unless something went wrong with the attack the US Army's 160th was about to unleash at the heart of the pass.

A ground team, probably from the 75th Rangers, had been dumped in this barren wasteland a week before to do recon. And for tonight, they'd reported a massive convoy of munitions crossing this disused pass from Jalalabad, Pakistan, to supply the Taliban forces inside Afghanistan. With the drawdown of US troops, the Taliban were gearing up to hit the Afghani government forces and hit them hard. Special Ops Forces' job tonight was to make sure the Talies didn't receive the supplies from the ever-so-innocent Pakistanis.

"Keeping chill?" she asked her crew.

"Chill," Dusty replied from his copilot's seat beside her. He'd been a backender, only recently jumped from a back-seat gunner crew chief to front-seat copilot, and they were rotating him through the different helos for cross-training. He normally flew troop transport but had logged time in the heavy weapons DAP version of the Black Hawk, as well. Now that it was nearing his last flight in CSAR, she'd definitely miss him. It was tradition to scoff at backenders who aspired to be pilots, but Dusty definitely had what it took.

"We be very cool, Superwoman," Chuff and Hi-Gear answered from their crew chief positions right behind the pilots' seats.

Her nickname had been inevitable. Being named for both of Superman's girlfriends, Lois Lane and Lana Lang, had labeled her for life. Her mother had always been a crack up, right to her last comment from her death bed, "Flying out now, honey." The fact that Lois had the same light build, narrow face, and straight dark hair as Margot Kidder—who'd played Lois in the old *Superman* movies—didn't help matters.

The two crew chiefs sat in back-to-back seats facing sideways out either side of the helicopter. Steerable M134 miniguns were mounted right in front of them.

The days of the UH-1 Huey medical helos with the big white square and red cross painted on their unarmed bellies were long gone. Bad guys now thought the red crosses made for good targets. And in the modern world of strike-and-retreat tactics, there was no quiet after-the-battle moment when it would be safe to go in and gather the wounded.

Rescue ops now happened right in the heart of the fray, and a medical helicopter arrived ready to both save lives and deliver death simultaneously. Some of the old-guard guys complained about that but not SOAR. The 160th Special Operations Aviation Regiment had flown into Takur Ghar, bin Laden's compound, and a thousand other hellholes, and CSAR crews like hers had been there to pull the lead crews back out when things went bad.

The two medics, a couple of new guys, checked in with her as well. They were the real crazies: Chuck and Noreen. They went into a hot battle zone armed with a stretcher and a medical bag. Beyond crazy.

"Thirty seconds," she called as the mission clock continued counting down to 0200. The Night Stalkers, as everyone called the 160th SOAR, ruled the night. "Death Waits in the Dark" was their main motto, and they did. They were the most highly trained helicopter pilots in any military, and she'd busted her ass for eight years to fly with them, spent two more years in training, and had now been in the air with them for two more. It was her single finest achievement.

Even five miles out, the flash of the first strike was a clear streak across the infrared night-vision image projected on her helmet's visor. The resulting explosion was small. The night's mission brief had said to stop the convoy, gather intelligence, then destroy the munitions. So, first strike had been merely to stop the gunrunners' forward progress and get their attention.

The latter part definitely worked. Fire raked skyward and not just little stuff. She could see anti-aircraft tracers arcing upward in a white-hot trail of glowing phosphors and hoped that no one was in the way.

"Stay sharp," she warned herself and her crew. The fire show was a distraction for others to worry about. Their worry was—

"CSAR 4. Immediate extract. Grid 37," Archie, the air mission commander called in. He was back at their helibase a hundred miles into Pakistan, watching their world from an MQ-1C Gray Eagle drone circling another fifteen thousand feet above them.

She acknowledged and dove for the dirt roadway. Grid 37 was right in the gut of the pass, so coming in high was just asking for trouble with the on-going battle she could see still in progress. At five feet above Lataband Pass, she unleashed the five thousand horsepower of the twin GE turbine engines. Fifteen thousand pounds of Black Hawk helicopter flung itself toward the battle at two hundred miles an hour. Even with the twists and turns of the narrow gravel road winding between the steep peaks, they were just two minutes out.

These were always the fastest and the slowest two minutes of her life. At her present altitude and the narrow valley she was flying in, even a stray boulder was a life-threatening hazard. Constant adjustments were needed to crest every rise and take advantage of every little dip. This is what SOAR trained for: flying nap-of-the-Earth to come out of nowhere, in the dead of night, exactly on target and on time.

Yet every second that ticked by, someone lay on the battlefield fighting to stay alive long enough to be rescued. She drove the turbines another couple RPMs closer to yellow-line on the engine's tachometers.

This time the faster feeling won out, and they were on the battlefield with a shocking abruptness. And battle was definitely the operative word. Her tactical display showed two Black Hawks and two of the vicious Little Birds dancing across the sky. But there had been three Little Bird helicopters when they left the airbase.

Grid 37.

Pulling back on the cyclic control to right between her knees for a hard flare dumped speed. Pulling up on the collective along the left side of her seat gained just enough altitude to keep her tail rotor out of the dirt as she slowed. She hammered them down less than a hundred feet from the crumpled remains of the Little Bird helicopter.

Everything was happening at once. Chuff and Hi-Gear were already laying down covering fire, their miniguns blazing with a dragon's deep-throated roar. At three thousand rounds a minute, they scorched the earth anywhere they spotted a bad guy. Chuck and Noreen were already out at a dead sprint toward the crumpled helo.

She debated pulling back aloft to offer them better cover, but the intensity of the overhead air battle told her if she went aloft, she'd have to move well out of the area to be of any use. Her people stood a better chance if she stayed on the ground.

So instead, she remained a sitting duck in the heart of Grid 37 and counted the seconds. A hundred-foot sprint, with heavy gear but high adrenaline: ten seconds. If the injured weren't trapped but perhaps delirious enough with pain to fight against rescue: thirty seconds to get them strapped down. A hundred-foot return carrying deadweight on a stretcher or slow-limping someone back to her aircraft: twenty seconds more. If they were bloody lucky, they only had to survive one minute beneath the tracer-lit madness so close above them.

Rather than watch the medics, she watched the tactical displays. She was getting heavy cover from above. A technical appeared from nowhere around an outcrop: a Toyota pickup with a heavy-caliber machine gun mounted on the bed—serious nightmare vehicle. But Hi-Gear was on it, and in moments the truck was adding its own fireball plume to the light and confusion of the night.

"Ten," one of the medics shouted.

Lois shifted from counting up seconds—she'd only reached forty so they were ten full seconds ahead of her best estimate—to counting them down. She eased up on the collective until the helicopter was dancing on the dirt in its eagerness to be aloft.

She ignored the bright sparks of bullets pinging off her forward windscreen, hoping nothing was a big enough caliber to punch through. Her audio-based threat detector filling her ears with muted squeals indicating only small-arms fire; the big stuff was still hunting the SOAR attackers overhead. The directional microphones translated each bullet's trajectory into fire-return data, and her crew chiefs were pounding back on those positions.

At five seconds to go, a crowd came out of the roiling dust kicked up by her rotors.

She glanced over for just an instant and then returned her attention to tactical while her mind unraveled what she'd just seen.

One medic carrying a man over his shoulder, dead-man style. The second medic pulled one end of a stretcher, the other end dragging on the road's gravel surface with a body strapped to it; good, both of her crew accounted for. Two other guys limping in with their arms around each others' shoulders, clearly nothing else keeping them upright.

The last two deserved a second glance. MICH helmets and HK416 rifles rather than the FN SCARs that all of SOAR carried across their chests. Delta Force operators. If Delta were on the ground here, it meant this action was much heavier duty than she'd thought. That explained the unexpected scale of the firefight.

At zero on her countdown, she could feel the shift in her two-inch high hover as the team slammed aboard. She gave the stretcher bearer an extra three seconds to load.

The "GO!" came just as she racked up on the collective getting her off the dirt and airborne without a wasted instant.

Whatever was happening in the cargo bay was no longer her problem. They could do everything that most field hospitals could do. If you were alive when CSAR got you, your life expectancy was very high. And sometimes even if you weren't.

Lois punched through the dust brownout kicked up by her own rotors and headed back the way she'd come. She slewed hard to clear the first turn in the road as the battle behind her moved toward the other end of the pass.

She climbed enough to keep her rotor blades clear of the ground and leaned into the first turn in the ravine.

She barely had time to see the white-hot streak coming in her direction. "RPG!" the warbling tone of the threat detector screeched out. The rock-et-propelled grenade impacted her Number One turbine engine with no chance of an evasive ma-neuver. Dusty pulled the overhead Fire Suppress T-handle as Chuff's minigun announced he was taking care of whoever had gotten them. That was no longer the problem.

The problem was she was in a turn that needed four-thousand horsepower to recover from, and she now had twenty-six hundred. She cranked the Number Two engine right into redline and yanked up hard on the collective.

Available at fine retailers everywhere.

Other works by M.L. Buchman

MAIN FLIGHT
The Night Is Mine
I Own the Dawn
Wait Until Dark
Take Over at Midnight
Light Up the Night
Bring On the Dusk
By Break of Day

WHITE HOUSE HOLIDAY
Daniel's Christmas
Frank's Independence Day
Peter's Christmas
Zachary's Christmas
Roy's Independence Day
Damien's Christmas

AND THE NAVY
Christmas at Steel Beach
Christmas at Peleliu Cove

5E
Target of the Heart
Target Lock on Love
Target of Mine

Delta Force
Target Engaged
Heart Strike